CHINA SEA

CHALLENGER

Clive Hopkins

Pen Press

First published in Great Britain by Pen Press

All paper used in the printing of this book has been made from
wood grown in managed, sustainable forests.

ISBN13:978-1-907172-39-7

Printed and bound in the UK
Pen Press is an imprint of Indepenpress Publishing Limited
25 Eastern Place
Brighton
BN2 1GJ

A catalogue record of this book is available from
the British Library

Cover design by Jacqueline Abromeit

ABOUT THE AUTHOR

The Author joined HMS Ganges at the age of 15 and, in the following years, served in Destroyers in the north Atlantic, the Baltic, the Mediterranean, the Indian Ocean, the South China Sea, the Yellow Sea and the Pacific Ocean – a blue water sailor.

Since coming ashore, he has worked in Canada, the UK, the USA, Germany and Switzerland as a journalist and, more recently, as the organizer of international trade fairs.

Since 1999 he has been an active member of the Chatham Historic Dockyard Historic Ships Restoration Group, working on HMS Cavalier; the last Royal Navy WWII destroyers still afloat. HMS Cavalier is an integral part of the National Destroyer Memorial.

Also by the author:

Challenger's War

AUTHOR'S NOTE

In 2007, the government of Malaysia revisited the beginning of their country's independence and generously awarded a specially designed medal - the Pingat Jasa Malaysia Medal - to the thousands of young British servicemen whose continued protection between 1957 and 1966 guaranteed Merdeka (independence) and freedom of that new country from communist insurgence. What is more, and is particularly impressive, was the decision by that government to send a Minister to Britain to present (wherever possible) these medals personally; a truly magnificent gesture.

Prior to 1957, modern Malaysia's freedom from communism was fought for and established by the thousands of teen-age, British national service, temporary soldiers who equally proudly wear the British army's General Service Medal with its Malaya clasp.

These temporary soldiers, who were sent by a government that they were too young to vote for to a country of which few had ever heard to fight a war under conditions that none of them could have imagined, are now retired and largely forgotten. It is to them and to my friend John, who was one of them, that this book is dedicated. Without them, there would have been no Merdeka; indeed, no Malaysia.

I must put on record my gratitude to my editor Paul who showed me the errors of my way.

ONE

The adrenalin surge that danger always created was no longer there, nor was the cold sweat that gave physical form to the fear of the unknowable. The heightened awareness; the racing pulse accompanying a tightness in the stomach, impossibly combined with a threatened looseness of the bowel, was gone too.

It was over, the war was now far away and yet, for no reason that he could fathom, it wouldn't go away. He wondered about the others, he looked around him; he wondered if they felt as he did, still all wound up like a two-bob watch.

To Commander David Powers, sitting in his Captain's Chair on the open bridge of HMS Challenger, all about him appeared normal although, only days ago, the ship's bombardment of Inchon had been dramatic and dangerous. More than 260 ships from eight navies had made possible the biggest beach landing since 'D' day in 1944 and the noise and pyrotechnics of that battle were still fresh in his mind. He could still see it all.

Sneaking in total darkness through the narrow approach channel, secretly cleared of mines by his own divers only the night before, he had been in danger of running aground and losing his ship, and possibly the lives of all onboard. But that was war. That was what they did, that was what they trained for.

Now, here, he knew there was no immediate danger to his ship or to his ship's company. Half way to Singapore, to which Challenger was en-route for a long overdue refit and what the Americans called Rest and Recreation, there was no possibility of his ship being attacked. The Korean war was still a local war unlike WW2, in which there had been nowhere safe from attack by the enemy. He knew that slowly, both his and his ship's company's bowstring-taut nerves that had been tightened almost to breaking-point would ease. Life would get back to normal, it always did.

What he needed now, he knew, was something solid, something normal upon which to lay down for a moment the burden of command responsibility, to enjoy the relief he had felt at having lost no men and sustained little serious damage to the ship.

The officer of the watch could operate the ship perfectly well whilst the captain sat sunning himself, allowing his mind to wander where it wished. He allowed his thoughts to drift to the coming refit and the much-needed modernisation; to routine things.

Laid down in 1943, an Emergency Class destroyer, Challenger was one of many such ships built in haste during that war and many had been sunk before peace had been restored. How many thousands of young men had gone down with them, or died subsequently as a result of their wounds or ill-treatment as prisoners of war, was still a matter of heated debate amongst historians.

In the end, as in all those entirely predictable Hollywood films, the good guys had won and the bad guys had lost but things had not worked out quite as hoped. The outbreak of war in Korea three months ago had turned a peacetime cruise into a mission with an uncertain outcome. In Challenger, he knew, Able Seaman Arthur was not a happy man.

He had served his two and a half year peacetime commission in the ship and was overdue for repatriation to the UK. If he didn't get home soon, he had told the first lieutenant, even his wife wouldn't recognise him. And his baby had never set eyes on him.

Powers thought of his new wife, sitting at home like Mrs Arthur, waiting for a letter.

Like most sailors, Powers was in the habit of writing a continuing letter that he would post when the opportunity presented itself. He would suggest to Sable, when he added to his letter tonight, that she get a passage out to Singapore. Even if it was for only a few months, whilst the ship was in dockyard hands, that would be great and would give them an opportunity to have a second, more exotic honeymoon; he felt badly about leaving her only a few weeks after their wedding.

He had been married before, to the girl he still remembered as 'the fair Helen' and it still hurt when he remembered her. That had been in 1942 and they had been ridiculously young and madly in love in an insane world.

Helen had been helping to comfort and clean up casualties as they were brought into the hospital from what remained of their homes surrounding the Luftwaffe's real target, the naval dockyard in Portsmouth. Only later did he discover that almost the last bomb of the raid had blown the hospital and his beloved Helen to smithereens. Like Able Seaman Arthur, he

3

was pleased that his ship was at last on her way back to Singapore; he missed Sable with an almost impossible longing. As captain however, the ship's impending arrival in Singapore presented him with certain difficulties that Able Seaman Arthur would not have to consider.

Both he and the entire ship's company would have to transfer to HMS Terror, the nearby shore-side barracks, and his first lieutenant, Lieutenant Enders, Harry, was at this very moment in his cabin working out the duty rosters which would ensure the safety and the integrity of the dry-docked ship. He wondered if it might be possible to arrange married quarters there if Sable came out; a suitable hotel would be very expensive.

The big naval base in the Johor Strait, which separates Singapore Island from the Malayan mainland, had one serious disadvantage that had been demonstrated by the Japanese eight years before and was potentially demonstrable again now.

Originally, this behind-the-island location had been an advantage in terms of defence from attack by sea, but the narrowness of the Strait itself made a sneak attack by the communists on the mainland not just possible but, in the opinion of Commander Powers, almost inevitable. He would have been unable to resist the temptation had the positions been reversed and, he had no intention of allowing his ship to be left undefended should such an attack take place.

He wondered what would happen if, in the event of an attack from across the strait, he fired 'X' gun, the upper of the two after 4.5 inch guns? With the ship in drydock, 'Y' gun on the quarterdeck would be below the level of the caisson closing the end of the dock and therefore not available.

Was it possible that the gun's recoil would drive the whole ship downwards with such force on to the blocks on which she would be sitting that they would be driven up through her bottom plates?

He had heard of dry-docked ships' own guns being fired at attacking German aircraft during the previous war but Challenger was a lightweight destroyer, not one of the navy's huge, armour-plated battlewagons.

Challenger's gunnery officer, Sub. Lieutenant Paul Horton, the ship's youngest officer, had admitted that he didn't know what would happen if they fired the main armament whilst sitting in dry dock; this was not a subject covered by his training manual. It was his opinion however that, without the water to absorb the shock of recoil, they might very well shake the ship to pieces and, that being possible, his advice to his captain had been that it was probably not a very good idea. What if the forty-millimetre, quick-firing Bofors guns, mounted on either side of the flagdeck and on top of the centre island were trained aft to shoot over the ship's stern? There would be a blind spot immediately astern of 'X' gun but there was nothing that he could do about that. Why was life never simple?

Powers didn't expect the terrorists to attempt a landing or to try to board his ship but a quick hit and run attack with mortars from the other side of the Strait or from a high-speed boat was, he thought, certainly possible. He would just have to wait until they reached Singapore where he could discuss his plans with the base gunnery officer.

This far from land, not even a bird was to be seen. He knew that, in front of his ship, porpoises would be riding the pressure wave, weaving from side to side, enjoying the exhilaration of the extra speed that the ship's bow wave gave them. "Peace, perfect peace," he thought, "Christ, what a contrast!"

The sun shone and, about him, the South China Sea stretched calm and dazzling blue from horizon to horizon beneath a cloudless sky. In the autumnal conditions they had just left in the northern Yellow Sea the rig of the day had often been duffle coats and mufflers or oilskins; here the officers on the bridge around him were resplendent in their starched white shirts and shorts. To port, about five hundred miles away, the Philippine islands were bathed in the same brilliant sunshine and to starboard almost equally distant, the similarly sun-drenched peninsula of French Indo China swept southwards.

Although there was war in that unhappy land, a war he feared the French were losing, here all was at peace and his feeling of restlessness was unnecessary.

He glanced around him. He was only subconsciously aware of the normal noises of a ship at sea, the soft swish of the destroyer's sharp bow cutting through the water, a slack signal halyard rattling its block against the yardarm mounting; he wondered how long it would be before the Yeoman heard it and gave the Signalman of the watch down on the flagdeck a blast. "We're not at war now," he would tell him, "get it sorted!"

Without turning his head he could see the Officer Of the Watch who, whilst having total responsibility for the ship, was clearly aware of his captain's presence. To his right, on the starboard side of the bridge, the Leading Signalman of the watch occupied a position immediately behind the fore-bridge weather screen. From that position, he was able to keep a watch for other ships and receive or send messages via the voicepipe connected to the wireless office three decks below. There were no other ships to be seen; the radar would have told them if there were long before the signalman could have seen them. But, it was this normality, this routine that would slowly ease the remaining tensions that they all must feel.

He couldn't see him but he knew that, towards the rear of the bridge, the bridge messenger lazed as unobtrusively as he could; available to run messages if required but safe in the knowledge that this would probably not be necessary. He too would be appreciating their departure from the war zone and would probably be planning his first run ashore in Singapore.

Elsewhere in the ship, had Powers looked; and he had learned many years ago not to look too closely unless he actually wanted to see, he would have seen various works being carried out. There was never a time when nothing needed to be done in a warship.

Dressed now in the open-necked, light blue, cotton shirts and dark blue cotton trousers of their Number 8 uniform, the ship's company were happy to have left the increasingly cold and damp Korean autumn behind.

God help the poor soldiers ashore, he thought, fighting their way up the peninsular against a well-trained and well-equipped local enemy. A hastily assembled, multi-national army fighting an enemy used to and prepared for the deteriorating weather and all the supply and replenishment problems that that would impose. Challenger had done her bit but…

Powers' supposed reputation for, and experience of, covert operations had been noted in high places and that was why his ship had been selected for her recent clandestine missions; he wondered what his next would be.

There was, he suspected, another, less official but equally valid explanation for his ship being selected for such operations. King's Regulations and Admiralty Instructions, KR's & AI's, demanded that the ship's company go ashore with 'HMS Challenger' embroidered on their cap bands. Inevitably, ashore and after a few beers, this was regarded as provocation by other sailors; his ship's company had earned a reputation as scrappers and for taking on all comers, a reputation of which he was quietly, if secretly, rather proud. They were his men, real men, men who had and would again without hesitation trust each other with their lives.

On the flagdeck, behind and below the bridge, Signalman 'Betty' Martin was using a chipping hammer to remove paint from the bulkhead inside the signal distribution office, the SDO and therefore unable to hear the slack halyard block above him rattling on the yardarm.

This bulkhead would be taken back to the bare metal before being primed, undercoated and repainted as part of the refit schedule. Yeoman of signals Houser, his petty officer, was keen for the work to be started and indeed completed as quickly as possible so that there would be minimal interference with the routine of his office.

One of the less official routines in the signal office was for the yeoman to use the long desk as a bunk. With the door closed, he could take an afternoon nap; fresh air from the five punkalouvres in the fan trunking above the desk ensuring that his nap was both pleasant and comfortable.

It must be terrible, young Martin thought. Never mind, he would spin out this noisy job as long as he could just to prevent his superior enjoying his privilege. He discovered that hitting the bulkhead with the hammer made him feel better, the harder he hit it the better he felt; the 'worker's revenge'.

Had the captain looked over the back of the bridge, behind the weather break of the foc'sle, he could have seen the whaler, the ship's sea boat, on its davits. Shirtless, in the bottom of the boat, its cox'n lay, facing upwards, checking that all was in order on the underside of the thwart and, with his head comfortably in the shade, enjoying the sun. Had the boat's cox'n said it aloud, the Captain would have been able to hear his prayer. "Please God make me brown for leave".

However irrelevant in this latitude, a sailor's prayers were always the same. There were two others; that for an everlasting supply of free beer and that for an equally everlasting supply of free women, but this afternoon those were not being invoked, those could wait until they reached Singapore..

On the foc'sle, two members of the watch on deck were slowly chipping rust off the links of the anchor chain, prior to painting it gleaming white for when they entered harbour. That this part of the chain would be invisible under the water when

9

they anchored was irrelevant; when entering harbour, the whole ship would be observable from on shore and from other ships and all must be spotless and in order. Tiddly was the navy's word for it.

The Captain had not been consciously aware of these many, minor, routine distractions but he did hear the disembodied voice issue from the polished brass cone of the wireless office voicepipe. He watched the leading signalman haul up the little rubber bucket in which signals were transported from that office to the bridge.

Leading Signalman Hawkins unrolled the sheet of signal pad and quickly scanned it as he smoothed it on to the clipboard, before offering it to the captain.

"Signal from CinC, Sir."

Powers read it and, recognising the unbidden, spontaneous, spasm in his stomach muscles, passed it to the officer of the watch. He suspected that their relaxing sunshine holiday cruise was to end rather sooner than had originally been planned.

"I'm not sure I understand, Sir. Why do they want us to divert to there?"

"No doubt we shall be advised in the fullness of time but, meanwhile, ask Pilot to sort out a course, will you."

Hawkins smiled to himself. Having read the signal, he knew where they were going and it was as a result of the careful redistribution of such inside information that the signal branch was held in such high regard on the lower deck.

Pulau Redang? He must have a look at the chart before going below at the end of his watch. He just hoped that this diversion would not interfere with his planned Christmas in Singapore.

Christmas in Singapore; God! Inevitably, it would be the traditional roast turkey and Christmas pudding in temperatures of over 90 degrees with humidity in the nineties too. Still, it would be better than freezing off Korea and being shot at.

Of course, the communist terrorists in Malaya, being communists and therefore, presumably, atheists, might choose Christmas Day to launch an attack against the dockyard. But, that wasn't his problem; that's what the army was paid for. He would be enjoying his Christmas dinner ashore in the barracks and, afterwards, sleeping it off in his mosquito-netted bed; a real bed, a luxury remembered only dimly from his last home leave.

He didn't care how inconvenient that might be for the Brown Jobs, the Pongoes, as the soldiers were known but, anyway, most of the terrorists were up north. With anything even remotely approaching good luck, he would celebrate Christmas ashore in Singapore. There was a good Naafi club there, the beer was cheap and the girls were easy; he wondered if the girl he had met last time he was in Singers was still around? Nice girl. Not a good girl, thank God, but a nice girl.

He caught sight of the officer of the watch looking at him and dragged his thoughts back to the ship.

"Day dreaming?"

"Just thinking about Singapore, Sir. Don't fancy barracks though."

"No, not like the ship is it, not like home."

"No Sir, not at all like home."

Home to Leading Signalman Hawkins was south London, Clapham Common. No, not at all like home except perhaps for the trees. There were a lot of trees in Singapore too but, no, not at all like home.

The navigating officer climbed up the ladder from the wardroom where he had been drinking a mid-afternoon cup of tea and eating rather more of the newly-baked biscuits than was his proper share. He shaded his eyes from the bright sunlight.

"May I assume that our little holiday is already at an end, Sir?"

"I suspect that it very well may be, Pilot."

"A little unfair, don't you think Sir? After all, we're supposed to be on our way to be refitted, modernised and generally re-incarnated."

"God moves in mysterious ways Pilot, as does his assistant, the Commander In Chief Far East!"

"But, surely Sir, we're still technically under the orders of Flag Officer Two, in Japan?"

"You may take it up with him when next you meet Pilot, meanwhile I would like to get this ship pointed in the general direction for Pulau Redang."

He leant back in his chair, now completely relaxed; the post-action discomfort miraculously dispelled; he suspected that they had a proper job to do. It would probably delay their arrival in Singapore and therefore Sable's arrival but that's life. If he couldn't take a joke…

TWO

Molly Cho, bar girl and confidant of a much smitten Sergeant Owens of the Prince of Wales' Regiment, looked at the sergeant lying fast asleep on her bed. She was fond of Bill Owens, he was essentially a nice man but he and the rest of the British had no business being in Malaya.

Before the war, it had been largely accepted that Malaya was a part of the British Empire and that most if not all the major estates and industries had been British owned, although there had been the first signs of them relinquishing total control. Political parties had been formed and cooperation begun on the long road to eventual independence.

That was before the Japanese, regarded by the British - and for that matter also by the resident King's Chinese - as an inferior race, had defeated the British army so decisively.

Although now back and once again in charge, the British were no longer regarded as invincible and the so-called 'stay behind army' of largely communist activists that had spent the war years sniping at Japanese troops and blowing up Japanese installations was now encamped in the jungle and carrying out its own war against the Brits.

Bill Owens stirred. It had been a heavy night drinking with the lads, but he regarded it as his duty to introduce the latest draft of national service conscripts to the pleasures of the Orient, or at least that part of the Orient within the confines of

Terengganu. This small port on the north east coast of Malaya was not perhaps the biggest and best place to be but the beer was cheap, the girls were happy to accommodate almost any reasonable perversion and what the hell, we could all be dead by this time next week.

Molly made tea. "I make you tea, Bill. You want?"

He opened his eyes, stretched and sat up. "You're a good girl, for a bad girl Molly. I don't know what I'd do without you."

"You find other girl and make her into a bad girl like me."

This was one of their little jokes. Molly had been a bar girl long before Bill Owens had been sent to Malaya to fight terrorists and they both knew it.

"You go jungle again today?"

She knew he wouldn't be going into the jungle again for some days. His job was to train the new men in jungle warfare. Get them dirty, smelly and quiet so that they could set up an ambush across a jungle trail used by the terrorists. He rarely went far into the jungle himself, his expertise was far too valuable and anyway he had more sense than to risk his own life if he could avoid it.

"No Mol. I've got another batch of virgin soldiers to teach how to stay alive. I'll be around for a couple of weeks before I can risk taking them into the woods, they could get themselves killed in there and, what's worse, they could get me killed. What would you do then?"

She smiled at him. "I find nice soldier boy to look after me of course."

"Yeah, I suppose you'd have to. No Chinese would marry you now, would they?"

"I married, my husband go away."

So far as it went, this was perfectly true. What she had not told him was that her husband had gone away into the jungle to shoot planters, plantation workers and, when possible, the English soldiers that Sergeant Bill Owens spent so much of his time training.

She saw her husband only infrequently at his mother's house where she would tell him when the soldiers would come; English Bill would tell her when the next patrol was about to leave the safety of their camp and where they were going. She had only to ask. Not, of course, in so many words but he would always tell her how his latest 'boys' were getting on and when they would be ready to go into the jungle.

"Seven o-clock," she said. "Time you go home and let a poor working girl get some sleep."

He rolled off the bed, pushing the mosquito netting out of the way and dressed. "Maybe I should take you home to England with me when I go back."

"No can do soldier. Army don't approve of soldiers taking local girls back to England."

"Oh, I'd probably have to marry you first. How about that? Would you like that?"

"Don't know, maybe so. Now you go before MPs come for you, then you never marry me."

Bill Owens put his hat on and closed the door behind him. At the bottom of the stairs, the small boy who kept watch for the MPs smiled at him and took the folded dollar bill. It was only one dollar but he knew the boy kept watch for other girls both in that house and the one across the street. He earned about ten or twelve dollars for about an hour's work each morning, and when the soldiers had gone back to camp he ran errands for the girls. If the truth were known, he probably earned more than Sergeant Bill Owens.

*　　*　　*

On time as always, the jungle-camouflaged 15 cwt truck stopped at the crossroads just outside the town. It was unofficial of course but everyone knew that it collected the overnighters and nobody asked what they had been doing overnight. "Damn silly question," as the colonel had said on more than one occasion.

In camp, the latest bunch of virgins had been fallen in on the parade ground by the corporal, ready for inspection. They were dressed in their jungle greens and were armed with the semi-automatic Sten guns that they would take with them into the jungle at the completion of their training; it would be their best friend and their most cherished possession.

Old fashioned but still reliable, the Sten was much favoured by soldiers as simple to maintain and light to carry. The days of carrying heavy Bren guns through the jungle were over, thank God.

Very accurate and a good heavy weapon, the Bren could punch a hole through thin armour but was not a lot of use when you were trying to carry it through rivers or lying under wet foliage for three days waiting for the enemy to walk into your trap. The enemy would be lightly armed and would run like hell once the shooting started: the quick-change, thirty-two-round magazine of the Sten allowed what was called hot pursuit, and rapid reloading on the hoof.

The 15cwt truck pulled up at the main gate of the camp and the passengers climbed out of the back, presented themselves to the guard as pedestrians, were identified and moved off to their several barrack blocks; a regular routine. The driver, having identified himself to the guard, proceeded towards the cookhouse, for which the truck had, officially, been into town to collect fresh eggs, fish and vegetables.

*   *   *

With Sergeant Owens gone, Molly bathed before making breakfast. She quite liked Sergeant Owens but was always aware that Europeans smelled differently and that she could smell his smell on her skin. If this was so, so would her mother in law when she went to her home to leave a message for her husband. Her mother in law knew how her son's wife obtained her intelligence but she hated being able to smell the English soldier on the girl's body.

*   *   *

The fresh faced, eighteen-year-old soldiers stood at attention on the parade ground ready to be inspected by their new sergeant, Sergeant Owens. He would remain Sergeant Owens until he told them that they could call him Sarge or, if they were a particularly good bunch, Bill - but that would only be when off duty of course.

There was a canteen within the camp which served local Tiger beer, sandwiches, cakes and most importantly, the best Cornish pasties this side of Singapore city. It was probably best, they had been advised by the older hands, not to enquire too closely into just what went into these pasties but they tasted good and filled their young and constantly empty bellies.

Being a soldier had not been the first career choice of these boys but their government had decided that the army needed a constant supply of young recruits and, calling it National Service, had demanded two years from their young lives. As always, Bill Owens had already established that there was the platoon comedian, the platoon fool and the neither one thing nor the other majority who could eventually be made into reasonably competent soldiers.

The sergeant was good at that and, as he had once admitted to Molly, he was actually quite fond of these lads who had been sent by a government for whom none of them had voted, to a country few of them had ever heard of, where they would be required to fight a hide and seek war in a jungle that was unfit for civilised human habitation.

Owens himself was less than convinced that the whole thing wasn't a waste of time and manpower but, as a professional soldier, he would teach these kids how to kill without spewing up at the thought of it and how to avoid being killed by the other side.

To the professional soldier, to Sergeant Owens, it didn't matter who the other side was; in his time in the service, he had fought Germans, Italians and Japanese and when off duty, a few Americans. If the present enemy was Chinese or Malay or anything else, it was all the same to him; he would teach these kids to accept that whom they killed was none of their damned business.

Their business was to kill the enemy and, if at all possible, stay alive themselves for long enough to be sent home and back to civvy street; a civvy street in which their mothers would never understand, nor even be able to envisage, what their children had been through. It was enough for Sergeant Owens that the majority of them should get to go home and he would do his best to make sure that they did. He had never mentioned it to his officers, any of them, that, as far as he was concerned, saving the lives of these kids was more important than taking those of the enemy.

"Right, you lot." He addressed them, "My name is Sergeant Owens. You will address me by my full title and name until I tell you you can do something else. Do I make myself clear?"

"Yes Sergeant."

"Yes, Sergeant Owens!"

"Yes Sergeant Owens."

"Right, that's got that sorted out. Now, my job is to keep you alive long enough to repay a tight-fisted government for the cost of your training, food and accommodation not to mention the vast expense of transporting you half way round the world so that you can spend your old age boring your grandchildren with tales of high adventure in the jungles of Malaya.

"Your job is to listen to what I tell you, absorb it and act upon it so that you stay alive long enough to become someone else's responsibility. OK?"

"Yes Sergeant Owens."

Thirty voices responded as one, which pleased the sergeant. That was what he needed, to instil discipline into these virgin soldiers. A few weeks basic training in England and then on to the troopship where they would have been sick for most of the time; they were not by any means seasoned soldiers and certainly not yet fighting men. When he had finished with them, they would be as good as it was possible for them to be; some would be better than others and those were the ones that would survive to go home.

He turned to the lieutenant, saluted and reported. "Number Eight Platoon all present and ready for inspection Sir."

The young lieutenant returned his salute and with a perfectly straight face, observed that they weren't a very prepossessing lot, were they.

In Sergeant Bill Owens' opinion, the lieutenant was himself still wet behind the ears and knew little about jungle warfare but he too would learn and if he was a quick learner, he too might just survive to become a general in some future war, that was the way the system worked; officers and privates came and went; sergeants go on for ever.

*   *   *

Molly's mother in law looked at the girl; the expression on her face was not so much disapproval as sorrow. Once, long ago, before the Japanese had come, the girl's father had been an important man in their village. Not the Headman but a respected Elder.

The village had been some distance from Terengganu, the home of the many families providing labour for the nearby rubber plantations. Single men, rubber tappers and the labourers who dredged the river bed for tin ore, etc. had then usually lived in dormitories on the estates but, once married to local girls, they moved to the village and set up home there.

Molly's father had been a shopkeeper, providing all the necessary foods, pots and pans and the thousand and one things the population required. Not the least important of these had been the knives used by the tappers to cut the vee-shaped nick in the bark of the rubber trees so that the latex would drain out and run down the vee into the little bucket attached.

It was this seniority and respect, coupled with his access to and supply of knives, machetes, etc., that had caused the conquering Japanese to sweep him up and transport him to their labour camp. As a slave, he had dug the ore out of the riverbed to be smelted into tin, a material needed by the Japanese war machine. After two years, he had escaped from the camp and, in the jungle, met and joined a small group of communists. The so-called Malayan People's Anti-Japanese Army; known in London as the 'stay behind army', were being provided with arms and ammunition by the then distant British.

At first, when the British and their Australian colleagues had surrendered it had been very difficult but later, equipped with radios and sten guns, they were kept supplied with ammunition by air drops by daring pilots who risked their lives flying low over the jungle looking for the signs that indicated the drop zone.

Occasionally, the Japanese heard and saw these aircraft and on at least two occasions had managed to shoot them down. The pilot of one had survived the impact and had joined the jungle fighters as an unofficial liaison officer. After all, the British couldn't get him out of there so he might as well do what he could to ensure that there was good communication between the suppliers and the users of the supplies being dropped.

In 1945, the skeletally thin, pale and bearded pilot had unsteadily marched out of the jungle and reported himself to the reinstated local British Commander, who had no idea what to do with him.

Clearly he couldn't be accepted back into the officer's mess as he was so he was sent down to Singapore where, after several baths, a haircut and a very close shave, he was issued with new uniform clothing and put on the first available ship out of there. Had he remained, he would have been a very bad influence upon the young officers now re-establishing the British Raj. He had spent far too much time with the natives, possibly gone native himself. No. Best to send him back to Blighty and let the RAF at home sort him out.

Molly's father had not survived the war. Already an elderly man when captured by the Japanese, the time spent in the tin workings followed by the deprivations of the jungle had finally caught up with him and he had died of dysentery in nineteen forty three.

Her mother in law, once freed by the returning British from service in the Comfort House provided by a beneficent Japanese army for its junior ranks, had stayed in Terengganu and found the girl.

Molly, whose Chinese name was Sun Lee, had been freed by the returning British from service in a superior Comfort House provided by the same beneficent Japanese army for its officers. She had stayed in Terengganu and met Cho, a nice

Chinese boy who had been homosexually misused by the Japanese. Molly had married Cho out of a kind of fellow feeling rather than love. What was love? To a girl placed in a soldier's brothel, at the age of just ten, love didn't enter into the equation. She and Cho had made love once but it hadn't worked for them and they had not repeated the attempt.

When the English had returned. It had seemed natural that Molly would provide a similar service to the British army whilst her now elderly and infirm mother in law lived on what Molly could earn.

Unable to accept the return of the British, Cho had moved into the jungle from which, in company with some of the original guerrillas, he attacked the planters, the plantations and those who worked on them. He also had a personal antipathy towards soldiers of any nationality and was often the one sent to kill off-duty soldiers in the town as an indiscriminate form of terror. It was hoped that the British would go home if enough of their planters, plantation workers and soldiers were murdered.

Molly looked tired, her mother in law thought. "Does he hurt you, child?" she asked the girl.

"No mother, he is very kind and gentle with me, not like the Japanese."

"Then why do you look so tired?"

"He is a young man still, mother, his demands are strong."

"Do not let Cho suspect that you like this soldier, he will kill him even if he is valuable as a source of intelligence. You know that Cho doesn't like soldiers."

"I will be careful Mother. You may tell Cho that the new soldiers are just as inexperienced as the previous lots. They will be kept in camp for at least three weeks learning how to fight in the jungle. Sergeant Owens will tell me when they are ready to go out on patrol and perhaps where that patrol will go. Then, I will tell you and you can tell Cho."

"He was in town yesterday."

"Why did you not tell me?"

"You were sleeping."

"You must tell me next time Cho comes."

"Its not safe for you to know that. You might say something to your soldier and they would hunt him down like a dog."

"Perhaps you are right mother but I would like to see him occasionally. After all, we are married."

"Don't be silly child. You may be married but he lives in the jungle with other men and you live here with a soldier. It would be too dangerous for either of you to meet except on very rare occasions."

Molly drank the tea her mother in law had offered and nibbled at the little rice flour cakes that she had made.

"Will it ever be over mother?"

"No child. The soldiers will never go and Cho's friends cannot drive them out. One day, they will have to end it all but I don't think I shall live to see it."

"Sergeant Owens tells me that there is a new General coming. Perhaps he will realise that neither side can win and seek out the leaders to talk to them. Perhaps, if he asked them what they really want it might be possible to compromise."

"You are beginning to speak like an English. "

"He asked me if I would marry him and go back to England with him."

"What did you say?"

"I told him that the army wouldn't allow it, that we must make the best of what we have here."

"Good. Don't mention that to Cho if you meet. I shall say nothing."

"May I get you some shopping, mother?"

"No child, there is nothing that I need. I need very little now that I am old but I am grateful for your kindness. Go home, sleep. I shall not see Cho for some days yet. I will let you know when he comes."

*   *   *

Platoon number eight, with Sergeant Owens in command, marched and countermarched on the parade ground; turned left, turned right, formed squad on the left and on the right and generally rehearsed their military parade ground skills.

To the young soldiers, this had nothing whatever to do with soldiering nor with killing communist terrorists and was accepted only because it was inevitable and unavoidable in this strange organisation called the British Army. The constantly repeated orders to shoulder arms, slope arms, port arms, trail arms and any others that the sergeant could invent, had the effect of ensuring that these young men became so accustomed to throwing their weapons about that they unconsciously also became less afraid of them and therefore more adept at using them.

Two hours of such activity, even in the comparative cool of the morning, was considered sufficient and with a universal sigh of relief, the platoon was dismissed to make a concerted attack upon the canteen, a glass of lolly water and the longed-for cigarette.

THREE

The Navigating Officer, Pilot to the other officers, rolled the parallel rules across the chart and into the trough from which it could not escape in foul weather; he turned to the captain.

"Nice easy one, Sir, straight line on 225 degrees. There's nothing between us and the island so we should have no problems with traffic. Oh, and by the way, I'm not sure if you are interested but we are at this very moment above the deepest point in the South China Sea; the nearest land is just over two and a half miles away, straight down."

"Most interesting Pilot. I have to admit that, just at the moment, I don't know what I am going to do with that piece of intelligence but no doubt it will come in handy one day." He turned to the officer of the watch, Lieutenant Brothers. "Come round to 225 please." Brothers repeated the order via the voicepipe to the wheelhouse below.

"Do we know why we are to go there, Sir?"

"Not yet pilot but no doubt all will be made clear in due course."

"That'll be a first Sir."

"Now then pilot, let us not be too cynical on such a fine day."

The ship heeled slightly as the helmsman altered course to starboard.

"Bridge, wheelhouse. Course 225."

"Thank you."

The alteration in course would be noted by everybody; everyone would have felt the ship heel, however slightly and would know that there was something going on. No doubt, when he came off watch, the signalman would be able to tell them what it was. Everyone knew that they were on their way to Singapore for the much delayed refit and any change of course at this point would be instantly recognised as a deviation from the direct line of advance towards the dockyard and, more importantly, the fleshpots of Singapore itself; Able Seaman Arthur would not be pleased!

*   *   *

In Challenger's wireless office, three decks below the bridge, the duty telegraphists, known individually to everyone as Sparks, sat physically attached to their wireless receivers by long-corded earphones. Much admired by the other ratings, the sparkers could sit there, hour after hour, reading incoming Morse code through the earphones and typing it in English directly onto a signal sheet for delivery to the bridge. A carbon of each signal was, of course, placed on the file marked with its date and time of receipt and the operator's initials.

Petty Officer Telegraphist 'Gene' Autry examined the coded signal placed before him before sending it up to the Communications Officer to decode. No doubt, this would explain the previous signal ordering the alteration in course. He called up the voice pipe.

"Bridge, wireless office. Coded signal down here from CinC."

On the bridge, the leading signalman told the captain who, in turn, turned to the pilot. "OK Pilot, you're the cryptology expert, off you go. See what the great man wants us to do. I imagine that's the signal we've been waiting for. I'll be in my cabin when you've sorted it out."

*   *   *

The junk, its bamboo slatted sails catching what little wind there was, coasted slowly across the calm sea. The smells of old wood and rope mingled with those of the innumerable and varied cargoes it had carried since it had first tasted water in the nineteen thirties. Then, she had been the pride of the fleet owned by the Hsu San brothers in Hong Kong but the brothers were no more, having fallen foul of the Japanese co-prosperity zone authorities. The ship, the Flying Tiger, had been pressed into their service until abandoned in Haiphong at war's end.

Since then she had had many owners but now she was carrying commercial cargoes from that port to other ports along the coast of China in one direction and to similar ports in Indo China in the other, with the occasional long haul to Malaya or even the Philippines.

She was one of a clandestine fleet of such old-fashioned and largely ignored native ships transporting Chinese manufactured arms and ammunition to terrorist cadres in the north of Indo China, in southern Thailand, for transportation across the border into Burma and in Borneo and to Malaya.

Outwardly unchanged since she has been built to a design itself largely unchanged in a thousand years, she could however boast two important modifications. Two powerful, supercharged diesel engines now nestled below the cabin on the after-deck, their exhausts covered when not in use by a hinged board. Flying Tiger was thought by her captain to be particularly appropriate name now that, if necessary, she was capable of outrunning almost any of the coastguard patrol boats she was likely to meet. Normally, her diesels were used only at night during which she could increase speed un-noticed.

A second, even less noticeable modification to her original design was the installation of a modern radar scanner within the large, woven bamboo chicken coop secured on the after-deck cabin roof. This allowed her to see and thus avoid detection by coastguards and others when close to shore loading or unloading illicit cargo or under diesel power at more than twenty knots, a speed that would certainly have attracted the attention of any coastguard or naval vessel in the area.

The only disadvantage of this useful modern tool was that, before switching it on, the chickens had to be removed from their coop to avoid being cooked by the microwaves produced. It had taken some time, when the equipment had first been installed, for the death of the chickens to be associated with the microwave signal but every night now, the chickens were allowed to wander free or were transferred to a smaller coop out of view from the radar.

Her commander, Lieutenant Wo, was twenty four years old, tall, fit and committed and had been an obvious choice for the job. Son of a successful Hong Kong sampan fleet owner, he had gone to the English school before, in his teens, crewing junks and at the same time studying and accepting the inevitable success of world communism. Proved at least locally correct in this he had, when twenty two, crossed the border from the British New Territories into the naval service of the People's Republic of China.

The Flying Tiger had originally been named to celebrate and honour the brave American fighter pilots who were then helping the Chinese to resist the invading Japanese army. It amused Wo that the name now identified a ship helping to fight American, French and British capitalist imperialism in the whole of Asia.

Tonight, having taken a bearing from the island of Con Son, a hundred and fifty miles south of Saigon, the Flying Tiger was steering 195 degrees for the island of Pulau Redang off the small Malayan port of Terengganu. Neither Lieutenant Wo in the Flying Tiger nor Commander Powers in the distant HMS Challenger knew of the existence of the other but it was inevitable that, on this course, given time, they would meet.

*   *   *

Cho entered the jungle camp having given the recognition call before approaching the position in which he had himself established a guard post.

"How many now?" he asked his deputy.

"Another ten arrived yesterday."

There were now more than a hundred men in the camp, a collection of small, stilted huts beside the little stream which, after providing them with drinkable water, joined the tin ore rich river that in its turn fed the lake beside which numerous rubber plantations and villages.

Re-indoctrination and self-criticism sessions, under the guidance of the political officer, were already welding these separate groups into a single force capable of acting together against the local authorities. Once the long promised and now anxiously awaited armaments shipment had been smuggled into the jungle and distributed to augment or replace their existing weapons the, by then even further enlarged, guerrilla army would break out of its jungle camp. They would take possession of Terengganu and control the surrounding province.

The British army would be both surprised and defeated by the size of the assault and leaders of the Malayan Communist Party, already waiting in hiding in Terengganu, would declare the province a People's Republic. It would be the beginning of the end of British colonialism in Malaya and a great day for Cho; the realisation of his greatest dream, a dream he would happily both kill and, if necessary, die for.

*   *   *

"Captain, sir." On the bridge of Challenger, the officer of the watch had been handed a signal and had lifted the cover on the voicepipe to the captain's sleeping cabin.

"Yes?"

"I don't know if it was important enough to wake you for sir but we have just received a signal advising us that as from 0001 tonight, we come under the control of CinCFE"

"Thank you." Commander Powers looked at his watch. "I imagine that the admiral will send us a welcome card shortly, I'll read it in the morning unless you think I should be woken."

"Yes sir. Good night sir."

He handed the signal back to the signalman of the watch for filing. Sometimes, he thought, you just can't get it right. The CinC was the Admiral based in Singapore. If he sends you a signal, you report it, whatever it might say.

Actually, the captain hadn't been asleep, not even in bed. He was sitting at the tiny desk adding today's instalment to his letter to Sable, but the officer of the watch couldn't have known that.

FOUR

There being no known, immediate, close or medium range danger to the ship, Challenger's radar was on a long range setting. Commander Powers felt no need to be on the bridge where the officer of the watch was perfectly capable of looking after his ship.

The letter was once more in front of him and he had told Sable that all was well; that nothing of any importance was likely to happen in the next twenty four hours but that, after that, they hoped to anchor in the bay at Redang island and pretend that they had come for a swim. All they wanted to do was have a beach picnic and, perhaps, organise a party onboard for the villager's children as the ship had done once before; before he had taken command. Just a goodwill gesture.

Of course, it wouldn't be quite that simple. According to reports, the terrorists were using the island. If so, then he would have to extract the maximum possible intelligence from the village elders without putting them into personal danger nor tipping them off to his intentions.

He was pretty sure that the elders were not themselves terrorists nor even terrorist supporters but in the real world, in realpolitic, the elders would need to keep both sides sweet if their village was to survive and they were to keep their lives.

His head drooped. He would turn in soon, to sleep, perchance to dream about her; about them. What would they do when he got home in about two years time; perhaps they would start a family? He wondered if she could wait that long. He had thought of that with Helen but the German bomber had intervened and whilst there was no risk of Sable meeting a similar end, time was moving on. Perhaps he should do something about it.

He wrote, "I hope that, soon, it might be possible for you to come out here and take up quarters in Singapore. I hope that, once we are refitted, we shall be left working out of Singapore rather than sent back up north to Sasebo in Japan, our temporary base.

There is now, I think, very little left for the navy to do in Korea. Constant patrols will keep the North's people ashore where they are happiest anyway and that will require fewer ships than are now based up there. The Yanks seem to want all the credit so they can do all the work, say I! Then we can be together again as we should be, you cannot imagine how much I miss you, even when we are busy playing sailors. God bless you and keep you, darling".

He folded the letter and replaced it in its drawer. He would be able to post it in a few days. He glanced at the bulkhead clock. Almost one o-clock; it had been a long day.

*   *   *

In the Flying Tiger, the radar was also set to long range but Challenger's masthead-mounted scanner was some sixty feet higher than the chicken coop on top of the junk's after cabin and therefore had the advantage.

"Bridge, Plot. Contact bearing 004."The operator on watch in his darkened cubbyhole in the Plot office on the deck below the bridge marked the contact's position on the Perspex cover of the screen with the Chinagraph pencil. "Range maximum, course closing, speed not yet established."

"Thank you Plot." The officer of the watch leant over the voicepipe.

"Any reason to take notice of it?"

"No idea yet Sir, I'm watching it."

"Thank you. Keep an eye on it but I don't suppose its anything we need to worry about out here."

At three o-clock in the morning, there was no way he was going to call the captain to tell him that there was an unidentified radar contact twenty-odd miles to the north of them. There was no reason to suppose that it wasn't some perfectly ordinary merchant ship going about its lawful occasions, as the phrase goes.

Disturbed from the reverie in which he had been sunk before the call however, he pulled the packet of cigarettes from his pocket and lit one. No need for him not to do so. The ship was not blacked out and no doubt, in many areas of the ship that he couldn't see from the bridge, other watchkeepers were smoking to help keep themselves awake.

In his corner on the right of the bridge, the signalman of the watch would very much have liked to light up himself but that was not allowed. Smoking on watch was forbidden; except, of course, for the officer of the watch and even he wouldn't smoke if the captain were on the bridge.

"Bridge, Plot. Contact continuing to close. Course 200 degrees, speed twenty knots."

"Thank you Plot. Keep me advised."

Twenty knots. That was pretty fast for any of the merchant ships he would have expected to meet here. Twelve, possibly fifteen flat out but twenty was fast. If it wasn't a merchant ship then, what could it be?

"Plot, Bridge. Range of contact?"

"Contact range eighteen miles but there's something a bit funny about it, Sir."

"Funny?"

"When I first spotted it, it was doing twenty knots or perhaps a little more. Now it's down to about four or five."

"And what significance do you attached to this remarkable change of its rate of advance."

Supercilious prat, the radar operator thought. "That's what's funny about it, Sir. I can offer no sensible explanation."

"Then presumably you were mistaken in your first assessment."

"No, Sir. I was not."

"Well, I'm not going to wake the captain because you think the contact has slowed down. As you said, it was at maximum range, you must have been mistaken."

"Contact now falling astern. At our present speed, it should disappear in the next few minutes."

"Thank you Plot. Keep your eye on it."

Leading Signalman Hawkins had his binoculars on the bearing but could see nothing. No navigation lights, nothing. Of course, at that range he was probably too low down to see the contact anyway. He swept the horizon from amidships to the starboard quarter. Nothing. Anyone being even half way civilised would be at home in bed at three o'clock in the morning.

He sometimes wondered why he had joined the navy, it was a damned silly way to earn a living but he was only twenty one and had already seen most of the world, so perhaps there was something in it.

He had been just fifteen when he had joined HMS Ganges, the shore training establishment - stone frigate - where the navy trained its youngest entrants. Less than two years later, he had been drafted to the almost new destroyer HMS Gabbard and sent to the Mediterranean. She had been a good ship. A good sea boat, not too lively and she had been a joy to behold.

Sleek, armed with four twin, fully turreted 4.5 inch calibre guns, two for'ard and two aft, twice what the poor old Challenger could muster, plenty of anti-aircraft armament and torpedo tubes amidships, the designers had learned their lessons during World War Two. By 1945, when Gabbard had been commissioned, she and her sister Battle Class ships were the best in the world. Not like this old tub.

"Bridge, Plot. Lost contact on bearing 045."

"Thank you Plot."

Down below, the radar operator had already entered the contact in his log and included the information that, on first detection, the contact had been doing about twenty knots but that, ten minutes later, it had suddenly reduced to about four. Let the petty officer sort that out with the captain in the morning if they didn't like it. Another twenty minutes and it would be four o'clock and the morning watch would take over. He could go to his hammock and crash. With a little luck, he would get almost three hours sleep before some idiot woke him up.

On the bridge, Lieutenant Evans entered the contact in his log and prepared to hand over to the first lieutenant who, when not in a war zone, kept the morning watch. Hawkins also scribbled a note to his relief on the signal pad. Nothing seen, nothing heard, nothing doing, life's a turd. Then he scrapped it. If the yeoman saw that he'd go spare. Signal pads were not for the use of budding poets, he would say. When next he saw Hawkins, he would also probably say something like, you're supposed to be a leading hand now, Hawkins, get yourself some dignity! A great believer in dignity was Yeoman Houser. Knew his place did Yeoman Houser and, more importantly to Hawkins, knew Hawkins' place; one rank below him and in for a hard time if he didn't behave like a professional.

The black of night had given way to the mid grey of dawn and, eventually, to the pearl grey that preceded sunrise. The wind was negligible and the sea calm; it would be another glorious morning.

There has been a tradition in the royal navy that, at dawn, the ship should be fully awake and the guns manned in case some enemy had stolen up on them during the hours of darkness. Of course, in these days of long-range radar, this no longer applied but Commander Powers liked to see the sunrise and to make sure that all was as it should be.

"Morning Number One."

The captain climbed up the ladder from his sleeping cabin on the deck below and greeted the first lieutenant.

"Morning Sir."

The first lieutenant saluted. "All appears to be in order Sir. Sunrise in about three minutes."

The captain climbed into his chair and looked about him. The ship was on course, there was nothing in sight and, just as he glanced down at the speed indicator under the forebridge canopy, the bright flash of gold of the false dawn flared over the horizon and subsided again until, a moment later, the true dawn saw the sun climb out of the water and set fire to another day.

"Never fails to impress me. Perhaps I'm simple but I find sunrise a truly impressive and invigorating experience every time I see it."

"One of God's more regular and enjoyable miracles Sir."

"As you say, Harry, at least in these latitudes."

The day had begun. The first lieutenant had been addressed as Number One before being demoted to the less formal Harry and the captain had been saluted for the only time that he would be that day by Lieutenant Enders.

"Anything in the log?"

"Seems Radar had a contact at about three o'clock but lost it astern shortly afterwards."

"Something we overtook?"

"Log isn't clear about that sir. I'll check the radar operator's log if you wish. I'm sure that will give details."

"No, that's alright."

With light to see, Signalman Sallis looked about him. The first lieutenant had the watch as usual and the captain was, as always at dawn, on the bridge. He swept the horizon in front of them with his binoculars but saw nothing. Ah well, another lovely day he thought, then he remembered they had been diverted from Singapore to the island of Pulau Redang; he wondered why. No doubt the coded signal received last night had told the captain but, so far, nobody had told signalman Sallis. He wondered what was so special about that island. God knew, there were plenty of islands so what, he wondered, was special about this one? He walked over to the chart table under the forebridge canopy and looked at the chart.

The first lieutenant saw him. "Something of interest, Sallis?"

"Just wondered where Pulau Redang was and why we were going there, Sir."

"Its one of the islands, the major island, off the Malay coast between Kota Baharu and Terengganu. Now you know as much as I do."

"Thank you Sir."

*   *   *

Lieutenant Wo hoped, though he couldn't be sure, that his reduction in speed as soon as he had seen the other ship on his radar had been made in time to avoid any interest being taken in him. Of course, if the other ship was big enough, its middle watch officer awake enough and its radar scanner high enough, it was possible that they had seen him before he had been able to see them; they could then have been able to notice that he had been doing twenty two knots.

The other ship had been doing only about fifteen knots so it had probably been a merchant ship, one of the more modern, faster ships now beginning to replace the elderly vessels that had survived the war. If it wasn't then it must have been a warship and if that was so, it was almost certainly British; and he didn't want the Royal Navy taking an interest in him this trip.

The hold was crammed to the gunnels with arms and ammunition for a major offensive to be launched by the freedom fighters in Malaya, a major offensive planned in Peking and for which the previously dispersed fighters were being brought together. More than that he didn't know; there was no need for him to know, what he did know was that his cargo was needed if the offensive was to have any chance of success.

It was hoped, he knew, that the freedom fighters could take and hold not only Terengganu but the entire province for long enough for the People's Republic of China to be able to recognise them as the government of that self-declared independent People's Republic of Malaya and to offer its military and diplomatic support. No doubt there would be many more runs into Terengganu, using bigger ships, to bring in men and munitions once that was established.

Volunteers and supplies could be landed in sufficient numbers to extend the new People's Republic quickly and permanently. The British were finished in Asia, the Japanese had proved that and now the People's Republic of Malaya would explode the myth of occidental supremacy once and for all.

The junk heeled to the wind. In the light of the dawn, he could see that the sails were drawing well and that all was in order. The radar had been switched off and the chickens replaced in their roof-top coop ready for inspection by any government patrol boat that told them to stop.

Below, in the hold, the planks of newly sawn and treated timber were stacked ten deep on top of the military cargo. None of the police or military off shore patrols they were likely to meet would be interested enough to unload all that just to see what was underneath, even if that was possible.

No, with luck, they would not be stopped and if they were then he was sure that the number of planks that would have to be moved to expose anything underneath was more than the patrol boat's commander would bother with.

He glanced at his watch. Almost five thirty. He would receive his daily instructions shortly. It was just possible that his base would know what ships were likely to be in this part of the South China Sea at the moment. As long as there were no known military ships in the area, he could relax and forget last night's sudden need to reduce speed, inconvenient as it was.

He had hoped to be at the island by nightfall tonight but the enforced speed reduction meant that he would have to delay his arrival until tomorrow night. The reception group would not be worried, they were aware that deliveries could not be guaranteed at any given time on any given day due to the need for secrecy. They would be ready and waiting when he arrived and would be in a hurry to unload his ship and spirit the weapons away in fishing boats to the mainland; a combination

43

of bribery and threat would ensure that there were sufficient fishing boats to accomplish this within a couple of days.

At first, he had hoped to be able to maintain his rendezvous by increasing his speed again once the other ship had disappeared from his radar but twice he had crept up into radar range again and had been forced to reduce speed to such an extent that his arrival tonight had been made impossible.

He ate his breakfast, a British habit he had not been able to shake off and, lowering his head, entered the tiny cabin. In the corner was another hangover from his days in Hong Kong. An affectation he was happy to admit to was the flush toilet in the corner of the cabin. Beneath this very British invention was secreted a powerful wireless receiver.

FIVE

Sergeant Bill Owens watched his new platoon sweating and grunting as they completed the assault course through which they had to pass to reach not only the other end but, at that other end, their N.A.A.F.I. break and their cup of tea or glass of that diluted fruit juice known to all as lolly water; beer would have to wait until they had finished duty for the day.

Hopeless. No more hopeless than any of the previous groups of national servicemen he had been sent but, as jungle fighters they were nowhere. Not a chance. Absolutely useless! Only marginally better than the last lot who were now blooded by three deep penetration patrols and confident that they could take on the entire communist world and win. If only that were true, he thought, we could all go home; it would be Christmas soon.

In truth, as soldiers, they were rubbish, but they were British rubbish and he was the man to turn that British rubbish into fighting men even if it killed them; and he was very much afraid it might very well kill some of them.

This was no boy scout camp affair, whatever the politicians in London thought. This was war, real war, war against enemies who believed in what they was fighting for and that was, in his opinion, their most effective weapon. The self-proclaimed freedom fighters in the jungle believed that they were right, that they were destined to liberate Malaya from the colonial British. These poor national service squaddies knew that they had no business being here. Malaya was to them a foreign country about which they knew little and cared less.

The only weapon that made them in any way effective in this war of ideologies was that they wanted to survive and go home to their families and friends. By then, they would be old enough to vote at the next election and they would vote against the continuance of this pointless colonial war. God! It was like something from Somerset Maugham in the twenties, it was as if the World War Two had never happened.

Sergeant Bill Owens, professional soldier, would teach them all he knew in the hope that the majority of them would actually get to go home at the end of their national service engagements. He, on the other hand, would still be here; possibly for ever! If it wasn't for Molly Cho, he thought, he would seriously consider chucking it all in, retiring, taking his pension, God knows he had earned it; go home, get an allotment, grow things, anything.

*   *   *

Molly's mother in law served tea to her son. Dressed in white shorts and a white shirt open at the neck and with leather sandals, he looked like any one of the more anglicised Chinese inhabitants of Terengganu. No one would have noted his appearance nor regarded his presence as in any way unusual.

"When will the guns come?"

"They are expected at the island tonight. I have arranged for the fishermen to bring some in with their fish each morning so that nobody will notice anything unusual. The police here are not very observant and see only what they expect to see, only what they want to see."

"Good. It will be a great day when we liberate Terengganu and declare our independence."

"You are very brave Cho and you believe in what you are doing but do not underestimate the resistance of the British. They have been here since the nineteenth century and will not give up Malaya easily again."

"But the Japanese made them look silly in 1941, showed that they were just paper tigers, not real soldiers at all."

"That was then and now is now Cho. Do not think it will be easy. This is a new generation of British, young men hardened by war, properly trained."

"They are just temporary soldiers, conscripts serving for two years in an army they don't want to serve in and interested only in staying alive long enough to go home and forget Malaya."

"Very true Cho but remember, if you attack them, these temporary soldiers will fight you to stay alive. They may not care about Malaya but they care very strongly about staying alive, all young men do."

"You are right mother but we believe more strongly than they do and they will crack and run first."

"Then Cho, do not forget that you need not kill them to win the war, you only have to drive them out of Malaya. The disgrace they will suffer from running away again will encourage others to join you more certainly than if you have to kill them all and lose many of our own men at the same time."

*   *   *

"Alright you lot. Get yourselves back to camp and clean yourselves up, you look disgusting. You're supposed to be

British soldiers, not mud-spattered bloody coolies who've just hand pulled their first rice harvest."

Sergeant Owens was pleased. Not very pleased but pleased enough to offer some small sympathy to his men. They had tried and they had all completed the task without too much difficulty. Tomorrow they would move on to the next, more difficult assault course. There, they would face real discomfort and even a degree of real danger. They would be shot at with live ammunition. Hopefully none of them would be silly enough to panic, to stand up and run. The live rounds would be passing only about a foot above their ground-crawling bodies and if they looked up they would almost be able to see them; certainly to feel the wind as they passed. He hoped they were ready for it, he had done all he could to prepare them.

In just two more weeks, they must be trained and ready to take part in the planned offensive. It was, of course, a secret but everyone knew there was to be a major push against the terrorists. The police had heard that the terrorists were concentrating in some numbers in the jungle to the west and this platoon would be needed. It was his job to make sure that they were ready but sometimes he wondered whether it would be kinder to report to the Colonel that, regrettably Sir, the platoon was not up to the job allotted.

It would probably make no difference, they would be sent anyway but he might just feel a little better about it. He would have tried. Of course, he would be sent home but was that necessarily a bad thing? Perhaps he should think seriously about marrying Molly and taking her home to England and a safe life. The army wouldn't like it but the army would have to put up with it, they owed him, he had done his twenty two years and he was entitled.

*   *   *

The first lieutenant looked up at the knock on his cabin door. "Yes?"

The navigating officer, DeeDee Darling, was unsure but sufficiently puzzled to ask his first lieutenant's advice.

"It's that radar contact during the night Sir."

"You'd better come in and sit down DeeDee. What about the radar contact. I gather from the log that it appeared then it got left behind. What's the problem?"

"Well, Sir, it seems that it wasn't quite that simple. I've spoken with the operator and he is convinced that when he first spotted it the contact was to the north of us, converging and doing twenty knots at least. About ten minutes later, he tells me, it suddenly reduced speed to about four knots and slowly fell behind. The funny thing is, he's absolutely sure that twice he thought he saw it again, just for a few minutes doing about fifteen knots then it fell behind again; almost as if each time it spotted us it had slowed down again."

"You think it was following us but trying to keep out of radar range?"

"I don't know Sir. There's nothing on the radar at the moment but who would want to shadow us and why?"

"Perhaps we should have a word with Father."

The captain is always known as the father of the ship and good captains encouraged the junior officers to regard them in that light; someone to whom they could talk, from whom they could ask advice.

The captain's cabin door was, as always, open. They knocked and were invited to enter.

Powers listened to the story.

"It does seem a little odd, I agree Pilot. You're absolutely happy with the operator's report, I mean with the operator himself?"

"Absolutely, Sir. Oh yes."

"Then perhaps we should allow our minds to wonder who it was and why it would behave as it did. Suggestions?"

"Not really Sir. Why would anyone want to follow us? Its not as if this were a secret mission, we're only going to Singapore for refit. Everybody knows that."

"But we're not, are we pilot? You know and I know that that is no longer the case."

"But nobody else knows that Sir. And anyway, our shadow must have been there since before we got the signal sending us off on this new jolly."

"Then what do you suggest? How about you Number One, what do you suggest might explain this apparent shadow?"

"If I also knew why we weren't going to Singapore I might be able to contribute to this discussion Sir."

"Ah, yes, of course, sorry. I was going to tell everyone this morning. We have been asked to poke our nose into the islands off Terengganu, particularly Pulau Redang. Seems there is a rumour doing the rounds ashore that the terrorists are using it as a rest and recreation site for those of their men who get jungle fever or just get too bored with everlasting running and hiding. Also, the grapevine has told the police that there is to be a large shipment of arms and ammunition delivered to the island for subsequent distribution to the mainland. Then, after that, we are to join the army in a little party on-shore."

"All very James Bond, wouldn't you say Sir? Really, I mean, would they really have an R&R centre right under our noses?"

"Don't see why not number one. We have been known to take our jungle-tired soldiers over to Tioman island for a safe swim and a few days rest and picnicking. I heard that the army's senior officers have been known to take their wives and daughters there for a holiday, transport compliments of the Royal Navy. They use the old Alert as a floating hotel, I hear."

"Didn't she have something to do with the preparations for the Inchon landings too, Sir?"

"Yes, before we got there but she's back on duty now as the fleet despatch vessel, otherwise known as the admiral's yacht."

"Oh yes, that's right, Commander Akers got himself killed, didn't he?"

"Yes. I gather his Number One got the ship back to Japan."

"Did he get the command?"

"No. They sent him home and appointed someone else waiting for his bowler hat. The poor old Alert isn't regarded as a proper berth for an ambitious officer."

"Ah well, that was probably the best thing for him then, eh?"

"Yes, I imagine so. Anyway, sorry as I am for Dicky Akers, this doesn't solve our immediate problem. Who or what was our shadow?"

"Need it necessarily have been following us, Sir? What if she was just going this way anyway and decided to keep out of our radar range?"

"That presupposes that she had radar herself, which means a modern merchant ship and why would any honest merchantman want to do that pilot? We don't often stop merchant ships and press men nowadays."

The first lieutenant intervened. "Could our shadow be the arms smuggler? If I were he, I'd try to keep out of our way. How about asking the RAF to have a stooge around up there and see what there is to see. They don't have to make it too obvious that they are looking for someone, they could just follow a straight course over the area and then take a long curve before turning back to base."

"Good idea number one. I understand that they have a regular anti-pirate patrol up there. See if you can arrange something will you. You'd better mark the signal Immediate or those dumb bunnies at Singapore will treat it as routine and pass it on tomorrow."

*   *   *

Sergeant Owens sat at the table with a bottle of beer in front of him and watched Molly serve a couple of young soldiers. Though known as Molly's bar, it was not hers and the owner lived in a small back room from which he could observe who came and went and how much they spent. He was an expert at calculating exactly what each passing soldier spent and although he trusted Molly, he liked to keep his eye on his investment. There just six tables, but when the soldiers had been paid they provided a small living without his having to lift a finger. He for one would be very sad if the terrorists won and the soldiers all went home.

Sergeant Owens watched as she swept away a soldier's hand that had come to rest on her bottom. He smiled. Her action had been entirely automatic, she probably wasn't consciously aware that she had done it; just one of those automatic reactions to what must be a regular occurrence. She didn't have much of a bottom, not as nicely rounded as some of the Indian girls and, like all Chinese, she was small breasted but she looked alright to him, he felt comfortable with her. He wondered what she really thought about him.

They had been friends, lovers, for nearly three years now and felt comfortable in each other's company. Neither felt the need to show off for the other, to try to impress. In many ways, they were like an old married couple; he liked that.

He was dreading telling her what the Colonel had told him about the upcoming action. Nobody, nobody that could carry a gun would be excused. Everyone that could add to the army's firepower would be going after the terrorists. "Got to get the buggers on the run before they organise whatever it is they're gathering for, eh? You know the form Sergeant", he had said. "Shit or bust, eh?"

Owens hoped sincerely that it wouldn't be bust. Even if his luck held, he knew it could be both. Once in the jungle and laying an ambush or establishing a firing line from which to attack the enemy, there was no possibility of defecating in a civilised manner. You went before you left the camp and ate very little while on the move. Bowel movements were not permitted if only because the enemy would be able to smell you from a long way away. Human shit was not one of the normal smells in the jungle and such a smell could give away their position. The clever ones went to see the sick bay sergeant before they left to get something to bind them; they could always take something else to relieve them once they got back – if they got back.

In a way, he hoped that the terrorist grapevine would have warned them and that they would be gone by the time the army got to the reported site of their camp. Hope springs eternal they say but this time, he wasn't sure at all. The way the Colonel had described it, it would be a combined operation with the navy's big guns firing from off-shore and even the air force. He hoped the navy gunners would be accurate and not kill too many of his men. He would be in the jungle, he had been told, for at least six days, possibly more, so he had better be prepared; and so had his new soldiers.

Molly caught his eye and smiled at him. He returned her smile and saw that one of the other soldiers had noticed her interest in him and had bent towards his friend and whispered something. The other looked round at the sergeant and then turned back to his beer. If she was the sergeant's bird, they were wasting their time; better move on to the next bar.

From his back room, the owner observed the little interplay and frowned. The sergeant was a good customer but, alone, he would not provide the income necessary to feed the four mouths that depended on the bar for their existence and that included Molly; he would have a word with her when the opportunity arose. She must not show favouritism, she must smile and be pleasant to all who came to the bar for a drink or, if she did her job well, more than one. As he had explained before, the first bottle of tiger paid for the chair, the table and the kerosene for the Tilley lamp. The second was what paid her small wage and only the third contributed to his profit!

SIX

The officers were gathered in the wardroom, the only space in the ship large enough to accommodate them all. The navigator had placed the largest scale land map he had on an easel so that the captain could indicate the supposed position of the enemy.

"The proposed action will not take place until after we have been to Pulau Redang but will involve our lying off shore and lobbing a few highly explosive 4.5 calibre shells into a piece of jungle. The army want these close to but not too close to where, so the police would have us believe, the terrorists have established a permanent camp.

"The idea is to make it unnecessary, even unsafe, for them to leave and force them to stay there until the army arrives to sort them out. What the army doesn't want is for us to drive them out into the jungle where they will have one hell of a job finding 'em and rounding 'em up!

"As I understand it, if the weather permits, our gallant brothers in pale blue will be providing a spotting aircraft and even, perhaps, a bomb or two to liven things up even more. The idea is, I believe, to provide as many whiz- bangs as we can as quickly as we can so that the nasties stay put until the soldiers get there to offer them alternative accommodation."

He turned to the map behind him. "This is the estimated position of the enemy encampment and it will be your job Guns to ensure that we don't actually hit it. A couple of hundred yards overshoot should just about do it and advancing away from the camp should encourage them to stay put, don't you think? Our boys in brown will be scampering through the jungle in that direction, hoping to bring the Pax Britannica to the area."

Sub Lieutenant Horton looked mildly embarrassed by the off-hand manner adopted by the captain. It was all very well for him, he was the captain and could afford to treat the whole thing as some sort of pantomime, but to the gunnery department it was for real. One shell falling short could take out a lot of English soldiers and he didn't fancy his chances of promotion if that happened. His second ring, his step up to lieutenant, was due and he didn't want anything to jeopardise that. Not if he could do anything about it.

The captain continued. "Prior to that little action, which will be largely up to young Guns here, we have been invited to investigate this possibility that the afore-mentioned nasties are using Redang island as a rest and recreation centre in much the same way that we use Tioman. Now, you may think that what's sauce for the goose is sauce for the gander but it don't work like that.

"It is also suspected that the island is being used as a reception point for arms and ammunition being delivered from China and transhipped for delivery by fishing boats. Our job is to investigate the former and to prevent the latter if, indeed, it is so. Do I make myself clear? What's our ETA at Redang, Pilot?"

"Seven, this evening Sir."

"Right Guns, I'll leave the arrangements for the bombardment to you whilst the rest of us get on with sorting out the island paradise."

"When will we be required to lay down our barrage, Sir? You didn't say."

"That, Guns, is because I don't know yet. I imagine it will be within the next few days or they wouldn't have diverted us from here, they could have sent Alert up from Singers, she's used to this sort of operation."

"Ah, Sir, but Alert has only the one four inch gun. Perhaps they want a proper job done?"

"I imagine that they do, Guns."

The meeting broke up into specialist groups, each setting about the organisation of their particular part in the forthcoming operations. The captain retreated to his cabin to write another page of his letter whilst he could; he suspected that whilst there was nothing useful he could contribute at the moment he was going to be very busy for the next few days. Ah well, if you can't take a joke you shouldn't have joined!

Outside his cabin, Powers could hear the chatter of the seamen checking the number two and four carley floats on their launching ramp, making sure that they were free to slide should they be needed. Number one and number three floats, on the starboard side ramps would be being checked too. With only two boats, the 27ft whaler and the twenty five foot long motor cutter, most of the ship's company would rely on the carley floats for survival should the ship be sunk. There, therefore, never any need for the first lieutenant to remind the buffer, the Chief Bosun's Mate, to make sure that they were always ready for launching.

There was also the captain's favourite toy of course, the 16ft skimming dish motorboat but that would be of little use in anything like a rough sea. Designed for use in harbour as a fast run-about, its maximum capacity was about five men, including the driver. Perhaps, used simply as a life raft, it would be possible for ten people to hold on to the grab ropes round the gunwale; not a lot of use. If it got swamped, the weight of the engine in the tiny boat would take it down like a stone.

*   *   *

High above them and unseen except by the radar operator sitting in front of his screen, the aging Sunderland flying boat altered course to port and flew westwards across the bottom of the Gulf of Thailand.

"Anything?"

"Not so far."

The pilot answered the question without taking his eyes off the horizon. He didn't need to look at the controls, flying this old bus was second nature to him after two years based in Singapore. Usually, the 'boats' were used for slow, methodical, square search, anti-pirate patrols. The South China Sea was an area where for some reason, pirates still operated against smaller merchant ships, junks or, indeed, anything they thought they could overwhelm.

Today, the patrol area had been extended northwards to over-fly the navy ship who thought someone was following her.

"How about some coffee?"

"Yeah, OK. Give me five minutes, I just want to mark our turn on the chart."

One of the few advantages of flying the old Sunderlands was that when they had been converted for military use, they had left the kitchen intact. The soundproofing, insulation and all possible comforts had been removed to lighten the aircraft and thus extend its range and capacity but the kitchen had been left and the provision of coffee and the occasional bacon and egg sandwich was the responsibility of the navigator.

Below, the empty blue sea was flaked by the occasional white flash when the sun was reflected by a breaking wavelet but otherwise there was nothing. There was no sea to speak of at the moment but the occasional white horse suggested that, somewhere, far to the southeast, something was brewing and pushing a gathering swell before it.

"We shall be turning to port on to the reciprocal in fifteen minutes, Skipper."

"OK."

"I wonder if there really is someone following our gallant sailor boys?"

"As I understand it, sailors are quite often followed by gentlemen of questionable morals but, in any case, we should be able to see them in about half an hour and, from up here, we will be able to see anyone else who's down there. Then we can tell the ground what the position is and let them tell the navy. What they do about it is up to them, I should think."

"Would they attack the follower, do you think?"

"Most unlikely in my opinion. I'm not sure but I suspect that there is something in international law about unprovoked attacks on merchant shipping; even nosey merchant shipping."

The navigator pointed down at the increasing white caps. "Looks like there's something working itself into a temper somewhere Skipper. Glad we're up here in the dry."

"Ah well Pete, you know what they say. Join the navy and see the world – from close up! I prefer the more distant view from up here. Where's that coffee?"

* * *

Commander Powers, sitting at his desk, re-read what he had written previously, picturing in his mind's eye the woman he had written it for, the woman he had married. They had met and married in peacetime, that brief peace time that had followed the war time; the peace time fraught with the danger of a third world war growing out of the Soviet blockade of the British, American and French armies of occupation in Berlin. Happily, the Russian bluff had been called successfully and the tension had eased.

They had wed with the hope of a long, happy and peaceful married life, both aware of the unhappiness he had suffered when his beloved Helen had been killed. Sable understood and accepted that he had loved Helen and would continue to do so for the rest of his life but Helen was gone and she was now his wife and he loved her too. Then, Korea had happened; destroying in a moment not only their dream but the dreams of millions of people all over the world.

He wrote the date at the top of a new page. "Darling Sweetheart", he wrote, "it seems that we Challengers are fated

61

to be the messengers of the Gods again. Our Lords Commissioners of Admiralty, in the guise the Commander in Chief Far East, have decided that we are not to go directly to dock as originally arranged, we are not to pass go and we are not to collect two hundred pounds from the Monopoly kitty. We have all been looking forward to this but ours is not to reason why, etc.

"We are to divert to investigate rumours that the Malayan terrorists have set up a rest and recreation centre on one of the off-shore islands and are using it also as a reception and distribution depot for arms and ammunition coming in from China.

"The first I could accept I think but the second is of course more than my Lords Commissioners could allow, so off we go again! Young Guns is all excited also with the prospect of a rather interesting exercise in bombardment. The object of the exercise is to miss the target by a small but sufficient margin to ensure that the terrorists remain where they are rather than make a run for it into the jungle. The brown jobs will be creeping up on them and hope to give them a nasty surprise; unlikely I suspect in a country where you really don't know friend from foe but hope springs eternal.

"Interesting little problem arose last night. It appears that we are being followed but by whom and for what reason I am at a loss to even guess. As far as I know, there is very little in this area that could seriously challenge us if it came to a fire-fight so I have no idea what our apparent shadow is up to. No doubt, in the fullness of time, all will be made clear. This usually happens just that few minutes too late for us to do anything about it but that's life!

"Please write and tell me what is happening in the real world at home. I do so much look forward to your letters, they are all that keep me sane in a world that appears to be going to hell in a wheelbarrow.

"If that man Foster Dulles is right, we are in for another long war and I had rather hoped that I'd done my share of shooting and killing; not to mention being shot at and avoiding being killed. Even if we win, it could keep us apart for ages and I don't think I could stand that; am I getting too old for this, do you think?"

Throughout the ship, the ship's Tannoy, public address system, crackled into life; it always crackled when switched on, one day he would ask the chief electrician why that was. "D'you hear there. Hands to dinner." Somewhere in the ship, some sailor would be adding the traditional corollary of 'officers to lunch', whilst drinking his tot of two parts water to one part rum.

Yeoman Houser who, as a petty officer, had already had his tot of neat rum tapped on the doorpost of the cabin, his cap under his arm. "Captain, Sir. Signal from Singapore." He handed the clip-board to the captain and waited.

"Thank you Yeoman. I'm not sure I know what to do about it but no answer seems to be necessary." He handed the board back to the yeoman.

"Interesting, eh?

"Yes Sir. Perhaps we should look out a white flag."

"I hope that won't be necessary, what would the admiral say?"

"The admiral, as always Sir, is not here."

"Yeoman, you're getting cynical; you must be in need of your afternoon nap."

Yeoman Houser replaced his cap and turned away with as much dignity as he could muster; the captain was not supposed to know about his afternoon naps. The captain pressed the bell push by his desk.

"Sir?" His steward stood in the doorway.

"Ask Number One to come in, will you, he's probably in the wardroom by now."

He folded and placed the letter he had been writing in the top right hand drawer of his desk, he would get back to it some time.

"Ah, Harry." He handed the first lieutenant the signal.

"It can't have been him doing twenty knots Sir."

"Then, Harry, who was it? According to the RAF, the only ship within a hundred and fifty miles of us is one old junk. Now, either our shadow was an electronic malfunction, an unlikely possibility I'm sure you will agree, our shadow has sunk or, somehow, that junk can do twenty knots."

"That's certainly the logical interpretation of the information to hand Sir but I've never seen a junk doing anything like that, not even the motorised ones in Honk Kong."

"Then, what do you suggest?"

"It was a small contact Sir, could it have been a submarine on the surface, one of ours hopefully."

"The only subs that we have out here, as far as I know, are S Class boats and there's no way they can do twenty knots even on the surface."

"Then, Sir, I suggest that we find this junk and take a look at her."

"Certainly, I would like to do that but another possibility occurs to me. What if she is the bringer of the arms and ammunition we are led to believe is expected at Redang? Then she would be on a converging course with us and, I imagine, trying not to be noticed."

"Then why do twenty knots, that's bound to get her noticed."

"Perhaps their ability to see us is not as good as ours to see them, if you follow me. Then, they would go as fast as they needed to to meet their deadline and only slow down when they saw us. How about that?"

"It would explain the two subsequent contacts, Sir. But, of course that would indicate that as well as engines, they had radar too, albeit shorter range than ours."

"Interesting, eh?"

"Very."

"Well, she's almost fifty miles astern of us now and her course suggests that she is heading towards Singapore rather than Redang but we'll see. We'll slow down at sunset and see if she catches up and, if so, on what course. Ask pilot to come and see me will you. We'll need to brief the radar operator to be absolutely on his toes."

"What about our own rendezvous at Redang Sir?"

"I imagine that can wait until first light. If that junk is the delivery boy, he can't transfer anything until he arrives and we are between him and the island. All we have to do is sit there and do nothing. I think we had better darken ship at sunset Harry. Nothing to show anywhere."

"Bit Boy's Own Sir but I don't see what else we can do. I'll make the arrangements."

The navigating officer tapped on the doorpost. "You wanted me, Sir?"

"Yes pilot." He handed him the signal.

"Interesting, Sir. Number One did mention it."

"Did he mention what we propose doing about it?"

"Well, no Sir. Just said you wanted to see me."

"Who's your very best radar operator? The one with the most imagination?"

"That will be Petty Officer Primrose, Sir. He really loves that machine, reckons he can see a fish jumping at twenty miles."

"Then he's our man for tonight."

"Might I make a suggestion Sir?"

"Of course."

"What if we go right in close to the island, our image will merge with that of the land behind us. That way, he won't be able to see us but with our radar pointing outwards we will be able to see him."

"Brilliant pilot! Tell Number One he owes you a large gin."

"There is one small problem, Sir."

"Funny that. I had a feeling that there might be. What is it?"

"Redang is surrounded by coral reefs and rocky projections. Great place if you're interested in tropical fish Sir. We shall have to nose our way inside the reef and that means that, to be safe, we should really anchor, Sir."

"Let's have a look at the chart pilot. See what we can do, eh?"

*   *   *

The Tilley lamps illuminating the open bar hissed in the night as the night insects flew round them, Molly sat with Sergeant Owens.

"I won't be able to come out tomorrow, nor for a few days after that, Mol. The patrol I told you about has been brought forward to next Sunday. Damned cheek that, Sunday's supposed to be a day of rest."

"Only if you're a Christian."

"Yeah. I suppose that's true. What are you? Anything? If I'm going to marry you, I suppose I should know."

"Are you going to marry me? Will the army let you?"

"The army can take it or leave it Love. I can always take my discharge out here and then they couldn't do anything about it."

"Don't do that Bill. It's too dangerous. You might get killed."

"What, more dangerous than being a soldier? You have to be joking."

"But you never go into the jungle yourself Bill, you always train the young ones and send them. You stay safe in your camp."

"Yeah, or in your bed, eh?"

67

"I'm serious Bill. One day, the British will leave Malaya and what would you do here then if you were married to me?"

"We could stay here or we could go back to England. I can always get a job doing something."

"No, Sergeant Bill Owens, it won't work. You stay in army and out of jungle and I will stay here for you. Where are they going, this big patrol of yours? You won't have to go with them, will you?"

"Afraid so, Mol. This time the balloon's really gone up. Seems that it's to be a major operation. Army, police, even the bally navy's involved but I don't see how they can help."

"But I thought you never had to go out on patrol. Your job is to teach the young national servicemen how to be soldiers, not to go and get yourself killed."

"Colonel says that, this time, I've got to go with them, try to keep them alive, make sure they don't kill each other."

"I hate your Colonel."

"Not all that fond of him myself but, that's the army. What he actually said to me was that I had to go with them to make sure they all come back. He didn't want a lot of letters from their grieving mothers."

She opened another bottle of Tiger and filled his glass. "We go my home tonight?"

"Yes Love. Tonight."

*   *   *

With the ship darkened overall and with the sonar pinging on short range looking for reefs or rocks, Challenger felt her way forward through the gap in the reef to the east of Redang island. The radar, on very short range, was being watched with extra care in case the men on the bridge with binoculars missed something on the surface.

"I think we're safe now, Sir. We appear to be through the gap and according to the chart, there's nothing between us and the island."

The depth recorder painting a picture of the bottom showed nothing untoward and, according to the chart, they should be in twelve fathoms.

"How close can I get in, pilot?"

"The island shelves very steeply on this side, Sir. We should be able to get within a hundred yards of the shore safely. The reef is coral on top of a separate ridge of rock."

"Very good pilot." The captain bent over the voicepipe beside the binnacle. "Wheelhouse. Cox'n. Steer one nine nine."

"Steer one nine nine, Sir." The Cox'n put the wheel over to port and met the ship's head as it swung round on to that bearing. "Course one nine nine, Sir."

"Thank you Cox'n. Five zero revolutions."

He could hear the telegraphsman ringing the revs onto the rev counter in the wheelhouse and the answering bell from the engineroom.

"Five zero revs repeated Sir."

The ship slowed. "About here, pilot?"

"That will do nicely Sir."

The captain looked over the forebridge canopy, down on to the foc'sle where Lieutenant Turner waited for the order to let go the anchor. To prevent anyone ashore hearing them, assuming that they had not already seen them slip in behind the reef, the order to let go the anchor would be made by the Yeoman showing a green light over the canopy.

The foc'sle deck and the hawse hole had been lined with heavy matting and this well greased so that the anchor cable links would make as little noise as possible as they slid through it and down into the sea. It was just like the time in Korea when they had slipped into a creek to land commandos.

"OK Yeoman. Green light to the foc'sle please."

In spite of their efforts at sound deadening, they heard the anchor go and waited, hoping that no one ashore had heard them.

"Right Pilot. You can have Petty Officer Primrose take over the radar now. I want to know when, if, that junk approaches the island. Number One, have the motorboat lowered and manned. If that junk comes anywhere near here, I want to be able to board her. I want to know why she's carrying radar and is able to do twenty knots."

"Aye Aye, Sir."

"Lieutenant Brother's is in charge of the boarding party, make sure that his men are armed and know what they have to do. I don't want any unnecessary deaths either amongst out men or theirs, just in case they are as pure as the driven snow."

"It's all under control Sir."

"I know it is Harry but just make sure, eh? Just to satisfy me."

*   *   *

"Why are you rubbing yourself like that?"

"Got an itch."

"Let me see."

Molly looked at Sergeant Owens' penis. "You been with other girl?"

"Course not!"

"Then you shouldn't have itch there. Maybe I not sleep with you tonight if you been with other girl."

"I told you, promise you Mol, I never go with other girls. You're my girl, you know that."

"OK." She laughed, pulling the mosquito net to one side and jumping on top of him. "Now you show me how much I you're girl. Stick 'em up, cowboy!"

She pointed two extended fingers towards his head.

*   *   *

In the dark of the radar caboose in the almost lightless plot office. Petty Officer Primrose sat watching his screen; watching the cursor, sweeping round and round clockwise over the almost totally darkened screen. What he knew was behind him, the screen showed up as a bright green clutter of almost solid contact, the shore and the cliffs above it. To seaward, nothing; nothing at all.

On the bridge they waited, the captain sitting in his chair, the first lieutenant acting as officer of the watch although it was only the first watch, from eight 'til twelve; he usually kept the morning watch from four until eight when in a war zone, but how could anything as beautiful as this island be a war zone?

If they had closed up properly to action stations, the first lieutenant would of course have been below in the damage control centre but tonight, there was no need for the entire ship to be closed up. The gunners were at their stations and that was, hopefully, all that would be required.

"So, Harry, we wait."

"Yes Sir. Always the most difficult part but after hanging about trying not to be seen off Inchon, this is easy; there's nobody out there trying to kill us."

"I hope you're right. You don't suppose the terrorists using this island as a rest and recreation sanctuary have mounted guns on top of those cliffs do you?"

"I doubt it Sir. A bit too obvious I would have thought. Bound to get them noticed, wouldn't you say?"

SEVEN

Sergeant Bill Owens lay back, exhausted; the sweat running off him. God! That was the best ever. He had had some women in his time and he had been with Molly for three years now but never, at any time, had he had a fuck like that.

Molly lay beside him, equally exhausted. She had done her best, her very best for Sergeant Bill Owens, her sergeant Bill Owens but she lay there wondering for how long he would be hers. If he went into the jungle with the big patrol, he would be killed; possibly by her husband. That would be a nice touch of irony but it wasn't irony that she wanted; it was Sergeant Bill Owens that she wanted, she knew that now.

She should tell him that the freedom fighters were aware of the impending campaign and that they actually intended to break out of the jungle and take control of the whole of north east Malaya. She should tell him that, this time, instead of running and hiding, they were going to stand their ground and take on the army. Tell him that the jungle was their territory, their home for, in many cases, some years and they were certain to out-fight the temporary soldiers when it came to jungle warfare.

It was even possible, she knew, that if the expected arms were received in time, the freedom fighters could be attacking the army's own camp while the army was still looking for theirs. She should tell him all that but she knew that she couldn't without also telling him how she knew it. She hoped that it would all be cancelled, that the army would cancel the campaign and make the death of her Sergeant Bill Owens unnecessary; but she saw little chance of that.

The supply of new weapons and ammunition was expected to be landed tonight and distributed over the next few days and more freedom fighters were expected to rendezvous at Cho's camp for their major offensive.

Molly was fond of her husband Cho but there had been no sexual relationship between them. She had married Cho after the war more out of sympathy than for any other reason. He was a nice boy, much abused by the Japanese and he needed a steadying influence, someone who would care for him without demanding anything in return. They had made love only once, unsuccessfully and then forgotten it.

When he had gone into the jungle, he had not considered her feelings for a moment; he was quite incapable of considering anyone else's feelings. To Cho, getting his own back on soldiers, anybody's soldiers, was paramount and he would carry on doing so until there were no soldiers left for him to fight. She suspected that his primary reason for joining the communist freedom fighters had been to use their organisation to satisfy his own desire for revenge on anyone in uniform.

To the Japanese soldiary, he had been, simply a young boy to be used sexually and forgotten almost immediately. Perhaps some of them remembered him, now. Certainly by now many of them should remember him, he had infected them all with syphilis; the syphilis with which they themselves had infected him.

He had never told Sun Lee, the girl the British soldiers called Molly, that he was infected. Not everyone was infected the first time or, perhaps, they would be but wouldn't recognise the first stage Many people didn't, it was often just an itch, a small scab, could be almost anything. The secondary stage might be missed altogether but the tertiary stage, the stage those Japanese soldiers would be at now, after so many years, was almost always a destroyer of men, fatal eventually.

He was happy that by now, many years after their little bit of pleasure with the young Chinese boy in Malaya, many of them would be in agony, having infected their wives and, through her, possibly their children also. Revenge is sweet and he often thought about them; the jungle gave him lots of time to think

That was then and now was now and now it was the British soldiers that he must kill. At least, this time, he was a proper soldier himself, he fought with a gun and grenades and killed men in battle.

Molly slid out of the bed, through the mosquito netting and found a bottle of Tiger beer. She would give it to her Sergeant and he, being an English gentleman, would share it with her. She wasn't particularly fond of beer but that wasn't the point, sharing was the point; something that nobody else had ever done.

"You must not go into jungle."

"Sorry Love, don't have any choice. It's called being a soldier, you do as you're told."

"But you might be killed."

"Not if I can help it!"

"I not joking. Why you always joke when I try to be serious? You go into jungle this time you get killed, I know, I feel it here."

She put his hand over her heart where he could feel its beating. His hand automatically caressed her tiny but perfect breast.

"Don't worry Mol, I'll be careful. Nobody's going to kill me."

"I marry you if you don't go."

"I can't not go Mol, I'm afraid that's the way the army works. The Colonel says you go and you go."

"I know you be killed if you go this time."

"Now then Love, don't take on so. What's so different this time?"

"This time you go into jungle and stay in jungle, this time you get killed in jungle."

"Well, I suppose its possible Mol but I'll do my best to avoid it, you can be sure of that."

She snuggled down beside him. Soon he was asleep and she lay there quietly crying. Her sergeant Bill Owens was going to die and she was unhappy. Perhaps that was what love was, caring about someone so much that you cried for them. She had never cried for Cho. She had felt sorry for him but no more.

At first, she had wondered why Cho had not wanted sex but she had become accustomed to him bringing her the occasional small present but demanding nothing in return except, of course, the information she obtained from talking to the British soldiers. Perhaps that was why he had married her? Perhaps he didn't care for her at all. Ah well, it didn't matter now. She had found love with her Sergeant Bill Owens and now she was about to lose him.

She hoped that it wouldn't be Cho that killed him, that would mean that she would have to kill him in return. She would not tell her mother in law about the change of date for the big patrol; perhaps if she didn't warn Cho her Sergeant wouldn't be killed.

*   *   *

The ship was darkened overall. The deadlight covers of every below decks scuttle had been lowered and screwed down to ensure no light escaped from the messdecks or the officers' cabins, the tiny NAAFI shop – always a consideration as this was manned by a civilian – or the senior rates' and ratings' bathrooms.

Elsewhere, all scuttles had been similarly deadlighted. All outward opening upper deck doors were fitted with cut-out switches that would turn off the lights within if opened and the entrances from the upper deck into the foc'sle had been closed. There was to be no possibility of so much as a chink of light showing to seaward nor to anyone on shore.

Supper completed, the ship's company had gone to Defence Stations as soon as the sun had fallen behind the island, against the dark shadow of which the ship would be invisible. They had two hours before the new moon would be high enough to cast any light upon them.

"If we're going to make a habit of this Number One, I think we might consider painting the ship black instead of light grey."

The first lieutenant smiled unseen, standing beside the captain on the bridge. He genuinely liked his captain, which was more than could be said for some of the men under whom he had served. Commander David Powers was a man who knew what he wanted and expected to get it but had somehow managed to retain his sense of humour through his rise through the ranks. Standing on the bridge in the darkness, he could imagine his captain's grin as he had made the suggestion.

Up here in the dark, just half a dozen very faint and carefully shaded red or blue lights were visible beneath the forebridge canopy. These showed the giro compass reading, irrelevant as they were anchored, the engine revolutions, equally irrelevant as this indicator read zero zero zero and various other important instruments which, were they at sea, would have to be readable by the officer of the watch.

As far forward as it was possible to position it under the canopy, the Decca radar monitor showed the cursor's rotation through three hundred and sixty degrees, of which less than one hundred were of interest to those watching. Illuminated in orange, this also was dimmed to minimum brightness.

The senior operator below in the plot office would be the first to recognise the appearance of a contact and would advise those waiting on the bridge. Only then would the ship go to Action Stations. The guns crews would go to their positions on both the 4.5in main armament and the seaward facing forty-millimetre Bofors guns.

It was unlikely that these would be required but 'B' gun, immediately below and in front of the bridge would, on command, fire a star shell over and beyond the contact to illuminate what ever it was. At the same time, the motor cutter carrying the boarding party would rev up to maximum and attempt to get alongside and place the boarding party aboard the vessel whilst it was so illuminated and, hopefully, confused.

Simultaneously, the twenty inch searchlight would be brought to bear on the target vessel to hold it illuminated after the star shell flare had fallen into the sea and been extinguished. With luck this would give the motor cutter a point to aim for and ensure that the target vessel could not escape into the darkness.

Radar Petty Officer Primrose stared at the screen in front of him. Not intensely, he knew that if he concentrated too hard he could very well miss something. No. He didn't watch the cursor rotate, he sat back and observed the whole screen, looking for the slightest indication of a contact; that first sudden, tiny blip of brightness that would indicate that there was something out there.

Behind the shield of 'B' gun, the gun's crew stood ready to load the star shell into the breach and the gun-layer his eyes fixed on the sight in front of him, waiting for orders. Under instruction from the Gunnery Officer in the gunnery Director above and behind the bridge, he would rotate the handles to elevate or depress the barrel of the gun. His buddy, on the other side of the gun, would be ready to peddle the peddles that would, under local control, rotate the gun on its mounting; the gunnery officer had decided that local control was a good exercise as there was no frantic hurry and only the one shell was to be fired. The gunnery officer had also decided that, for exercise, 'B' gun should be manned by 'A' gun's crew.

*   *   *

The sun was too low now to penetrate the light jungle of the island behind them. The ship was herself now in shadow and was unlikely to be seen from seaward even by an observant lookout and that was unlikely on the junk.

The same darkness that was slowly now engulfing them was, ashore, more quickly engulfing the circle of stilted huts within which the guerrillas rested. For them, it had been a long, almost boring day. It was considerably less arduous for them than being in the jungle on the mainland and being either hunted or, in their turn, hunting the plantation workers or the owners. By comparison, the island was a place of peace and plenty; of safety and tranquillity.

Here, being under no threat of attack, the days were passed in cleaning the protective transit oil from the weapons that arrived regularly from China. In the last delivery, the wooden crates had been filled with semi-automatic rifles, the ammunition they needed and hundreds of dull green painted hand grenades that would be used against the army vehicles or those of the civil authorities using the roads.

The leader had been here some time now and had established a modus vivendi with the Headman of the village. The camp lacked nothing in the form of food, fresh fish being a daily acquisition and locally produced pork and rice ensured that their diet was both better than when on the mainland and sufficiently nutritious to ensure that, when the men under his care returned to the mainland, they would be fit and healthy and better able to wage war against the British. Anything special required, such as medicines or drugs, would be brought over from the mainland by the fishermen who landed their catch at Terengganu.

Evenings such as this were spent relaxing; playing cards or just talking. Occasionally one of the men would fancy himself as a singer and folk songs from 'home' in China were a favourite on those occasions, even amongst those who had been born here in Malaya. In any event, life was quiet and enjoyable, their only worry being the approaching date of their return to the mainland, the jungle and the war.

Three months ago, one of the resting guerrillas had decided that he had had enough of jungle warfare and had persuaded one of the fishing boats to take him over to the mainland; not to Terengganu but further north, closer to Kota Bharu and had disappeared. The camp leader had explained to the villagers that this was not permitted and that any boat taking his men over the water would be burned and the crew shot. On that occasion he had shot only one of the two fishermen and had not burned the boat but the lesson had been learned and nobody in the village would now consider aiding one of the campers to desert.

Tonight, they had eaten their evening meal and retired to their huts to prepare for their return to the mainland in three days time. Their own weapons must be stripped, cleaned and tested as would those of the consignment they would make ready for onward shipment. They would accompany them, distributed between the fishing boats, one or two crates hidden under the nets and spare sails in the bottom of the boat and they posing as crew, one to each boat. During the next two days there would be almost constant lectures by the political officer, designed to ensure that they were at the peak of enthusiasm when they left the island.

One by one, the lights in the huts were extinguished and silence descended upon the camp. Later, they would be woken by the noise of the firing of the star shell from HMS Challenger but they didn't know that and sleep came easily to the tired men with full bellies.

EIGHT

A light offshore breeze wafted the smells of the island over the ship and those on the upper decks could smell the light jungle, the greens of the trees above the shoreline and the long grasses that that came down to the edge of the white coral beaches where the rocky outcrops had made the little bays.

On Redang, there was really only one major beach, surrounding a wide, deep bay in the centre of which stood another tiny island; little more than a naked rock. A single tree, sprouted from a single coconut that had been thrown up by a storm high enough to remain in the crevice in which it had landed, gave this miniature island the name by which it was known, One Tree Island. Nowadays, visits by the Royal Navy were few but not all that long ago, they had been there often enough to give the islet that very English sounding name.

The bay, its small fishing village and its One Tree Island sentinel, was on the normally sheltered, landward side of the island and was the accepted anchorage for visiting vessels of any size but, tonight, Challenger lay at anchor on the other side of the island. Any vessel approaching from China would have to pass the position in which Challenger now lay concealed.

Dressed in their flameproof anti-flash kit, with a hood that left only their eyes visible and heavy duty flameproof gloves, the contrast between the gun's crews and the officers on the bridge in their starched white shirts and shorts was pronounced. There being presumed to be no possibility of any return fire from tonight's target, only the gun's crews were dressed as for battle just in case of an accident with the ammunition;

elsewhere, people were wearing as little as possible in an attempt to remain cool.

"Guns." The captain spoke into the microphone connected to the Director behind him. "You might as well load 'B' gun with star shell now. We don't know when our target will appear, if indeed it appears at all, but I don't want any delay when I give the order; OK?"

The speaker in the open backed 'B' gun mounting crackled as the gunnery officer switched on his microphone. "'B' gun only, with star shell, load, load, load."

For this evening's little operation, 'A' gun's crew had been transferred to 'B' gun to ensure that all gun's crews were interchangeable. Behind the gun, Able Seaman Arthur, acting as Ammunition Number number one, took the cordite cartridge from the port ready-use locker and handed it to the loader who placed it in the loading tray beside and behind the open breach. His opposite number on the other side of the gun took the star shell from the starboard ready-use locker, handing that too to his loader who placed it in the loading tray in front of the cartridge. The starboard ready-use locker contained one further star shell, 'just in case' as the gunnery officer had said but they wouldn't need that. The rest of the locker was taken up with high explosive shells.

The breach worker pulled the lever in front of him. This lifted the loading tray into line with the breach and the automatic rammer pushed the load into the breach. The rear rim bevel of the cartridge depressed the retaining catches, allowing the breach to slam shut and hold the load in place.

"'B' gun loaded, star shell." The gun captain spoke into his microphone.

"'B' gun loaded, star shell." The gunnery officer reported to the bridge.

"Thank you."

"How long do we have to stand here doing nothing, Hooky?" Able Seaman Arthur was in a bad mood. Indeed, he had been in a very bad mood ever since the alteration in course had taken the ship further away from Singapore and him further away from his passage home.

"Just about as long as the captain wants us too, I reckon Arthur and no amount of whinging on your part will make it any less so shut up and stand to, OK?"

Leading Seaman Archer, the gun captain, was as bored as Arthur and just as eager to get to Singapore but for altogether different reasons. Before Challenger had been sent up north to Korea, he had had a good thing going with one of the taxi dancers at a dance hall in the New World amusement park. As a regular, he got what he was assured was preferential treatment; first option you might say, when it came to her deciding who was going to take her home and the advantage of all that that implied.

Arthur, on the other hand had been the soul of rectitude, according to his own lights. Not for him the easy girls in the New World or the Happy World areas; he was a married man. He had satisfied his sexual desires by being an habitué of Boogie Street where the attraction, apart from the beer of course, was the plentiful supply of ladyboys, some of whom were very much prettier than the girls with whom they had to

Clive Hopkins

compete for the favours of the soldiers and sailors in the bars. Able Seaman Arthur could truthfully tell his wife that he had not had another woman in the entire two and a half years that he had been away from her.

Petty Officer Primrose saw it first, of course. At almost extreme range, a tiny blip of brightness showed up on the radar screen in front of him. He watched it for a moment. "Bridge, plot. Contact bearing zero four zero, twenty miles. Course two two five, speed twelve knots."

The captain spoke into the microphone to the gunnery officer. "OK Guns. We have a contact bearing zero four zero, twenty miles. What does your box of tricks tell you?"

"Got it Sir. Confirm bearing and distance. 'B' gun stand by."

Under the Director's verbal control 'B' gun turned towards the target.

"We'll wait until she is in range, Guns. I want her close enough for the flare to silhouette the target and for the motorboat to be able to intercept as soon as the star shell lights her up; say about five miles.

"Officer of the watch, have the motorboat cast off and steer 040 at minimum revs. I don't want our prey to be able to see a white bow wave heading towards him. I'm hoping that his radar, if it's working, is tuned for bigger fish than our boat."

"Very good Sir." From the back of the bridge, the OOW called down to the waiting motorboat's crew. "Motorboat away, steer zero four zero minimum revs. We're waiting for the target to come to you, I don't want you careering about all over the South China Sea in the dark."

He turned to the captain. "With luck Sir, if our boat is spotted and she is only doing a couple of knots, the enemy will assume that it's a fishing boat."

"Damn! I should have thought of that. We could have hung a bloody great light over the stern like the fishing boats do to attract the fish. Ah well, too late now but we'll remember that next time, eh?"

In the boat, the boarding party were crammed in like sardines in a tin.

Signalman Sallis had placed in the bottom of the boat the boxed twelve volt battery he would need to power his aldis lamp when aboard the junk; Petty Officer Barber was the leader and Leading Seaman Booker his deputy.

"Has it occurred to the skipper that thirteen is an unlucky number, PO?"

"OK son, who do you want to throw overboard?"

"You know what I mean PO, we should have had one more or one less."

"I don't reckon this for a party PO." Another voice.

"Keep silence in the boat. You can talk all you like once we're aboard the junk, if you can talk Chinese that is."

"OK PO. How long do you reckon we'll be hanging about?"

"Well, if the junk is doing twelve knots, and you've got to admit that that's a very good speed for a junk and we are doing about three knots in the opposite direction, we could be hanging about here for an hour but, somehow I don't think that will happen. Once the gunner fires his star shell, the junk will either turn tail and run like hell or slow down and pretend to be an innocent passer-by. At that point, we increase our speed and things could get quite exciting."

"OK if we smoke PO?"

"Yeah, don't see why not, they'll think we're a fishing boat if they see a couple of cigarettes in the boat. Not all of you at once though. No more than two at any one time, OK? And those two should be sitting in the stern where the fishermen would be sitting relaxed if they were just making their way to their fishing ground."

*   *   *

Lieutenant Wo glanced at his radar screen. Ahead, the island was clearly visible and, between him and the island was a small contact, probably a fishing boat.

With no moon yet, he could see nothing else and he tried to relax. There was nothing to worry about, his radar showed that he was alone out here except for the fishing boat which might, he thought, contain a reception party to lead him in to the bay. But why would it? He had done this trip before and there had never been a reception committee nor, he thought, had there been any fishing boats on this side of the island. Most of the fishing grounds were on the western side where the currents between the islands and the mainland provided ample food for the fish.

He glanced at his radar again. Still there, slowly approaching. Was that a cigarette he could see, a tiny red point of light against the blackness of the night? The hair on the back of his neck bristled, all was not as it should be. There should be no boat there, it was unusual and the unusual could represent danger. To Lieutenant Wo the unusual was to be avoided at all costs. He would give it a few more minutes to see whether it stopped and fished or continued approaching him. It almost looked as if the boat knew he was there and was steering directly towards him. As he had no lights showing, the boat couldn't possibly see him. No. There was something not quite right about that boat. He shouted to the crewman manning the diesels below him. "Maximum speed."

*   *   *

"Bridge. Plot. Contact has increased speed and changed course. Now doing about fifteen knots and rising. Course now 270 degrees speed still rising, now eighteen knots."

"Bridge, thank you.

"Director. Guns, let's have your star shell please. I think he's twigged that the boat ain't all that it's supposed to be. Target now tracking left and increased to twenty knots. Do you have him?"

"'B' gun, train left to 050, up two hundred."

The gun moved, following the target, steadying on the bearing given, the barrel lifting to increase the range by two hundred yards.

"'B' gun, star shell shoot shoot shoot."

The gun firing bell dinged twice, seconds before the explosion of the gun firing.

Above the junk, the shell exploded but instead of releasing a powerful flare which would slowly descend while illuminating all beneath it, it exploded in a giant display of sparks and stars such as one might expect to see at a firework display.

"'B' gun reload star shell."

The gunnery officer's voice could be heard by all concerned and the concern in his voice was noted on the bridge.

"What the hell was that, Guns?"

"Sorry Sir. It must have been a dud."

"Bridge, Plot." The captain bent over the voice pipe to listen to the radar operator's report. "Target altering course to port and increasing speed to twenty three knots he's probably heading for the islands to lose himself amongst the clutter Sir."

"Thank you Plot."

"Bridge, Plot. Our motorboat is giving chase but can't keep up Sir."

"Very good Plot, thank you."

Beside the captain, the officer of the watch swore. "That's all we needed, a dud star shell. Never heard of such a thing."

"Neither have I Taffy but you learn a little something every day. There's no point in the boat chasing him, its outclassed. Yeoman, see if you can recall the boat. Use the twenty inch searchlight to attract his attention. Our presence is no longer a secret, he must have seen not only the star shell but the flash from the gun that fired it so he'll keep well away from here."

"Stand down action stations, Taffy, we're almost certainly wasting our time. I suppose we should get the anchor up and give chase but, by the time we've manoeuvred out of here, he'll be long gone. If I were he, I'd head for the mainland and lie too close inshore where our radar can't separate him from the background clutter."

The first lieutenant climbed on to the bridge through the hatch from the plot on the deck below. "Had a word with Petty

Officer Primrose on the way up Sir. Pity about the star shell, we looked set to win this round."

"I'm not sure that our Lords Commissioners of Admiralty will also regard it as something of a pity but there's nothing we can do about it at the moment.

"We'll have to follow, of course, but it's almost certainly a waste of time."

"What do you think he'll do, Sir?"

"If he's got any sense, he'll bugger off for a few days, looking like any other junk and then have another try. He's got to land his cargo some time."

"What if we try a little subterfuge, Sir? He has to land his cargo in the big bay so we could slow things down somewhat by going in there ourselves on a courtesy visit. Chat up the natives, have a swimming party and all that. The longer we keep him away, the more anxious he'll be to get in there and get unloaded and away again. He might just get careless; we could get lucky."

"Might be a good idea Number One. There isn't really anything else we can do. You know the island, I believe. Haven't you been here before?"

"Yes, a couple of years ago. We anchored in the bay for a couple of days and did a bit of what used to be called fraternisation but is now called winning hearts and minds. I met the local Headman and we had him aboard with all the village children for a party on the foc'sle. Usual things Sir, lots of ice cream and balloons, well, blown up condoms really but the lads drew faces on them and nobody cared. The Headman seemed to think Challenger was a very good name for a warship."

"I think we might do that again Harry. You never know, we might learn something and it can't do any harm."

Lieutenant Evans, the officer of the watch turned to the captain. "Motorboat alongside Sir. Special Sea Dutymen close up for leaving harbour?"

"Yes please Taffy. Stand down Defence Stations too. There's no point in everyone hanging about waiting for a war to start when the enemy has disappeared over the horizon."

"Aye aye Sir."

The boat was swung inboard on its davits and secured; the boarding party stood down and the anchor party mustered on the foc'sle. The engine room was warned of the imminent need for revolutions and the immediate need for steam on the capstan to lift the anchor.

"What's he like, number one? This Headman."

"Nice enough sort of bloke, Sir. Speaks passable English and appeared to be popular enough with the villagers. The children liked him and that's always a good test, don't you think?"

"You're probably right Harry. I'm not exactly into children myself. Never seem to have had either the time or the opportunity."

"No, Sir."

The boarding party clambered out of the boat to be greeted with cat- calls and comments about being unable to organise a booze-up in a brewery. All these were taken in good part and a few remarks were returned about gunners unable to shoot any more accurately with their guns than they could with their pricks when ashore.

NINE

Molly wondered whether, if she didn't tell her mother in law about the patrol being brought forward, the guerrillas in the jungle would not know when the soldiers were coming and wouldn't be able to kill her Sergeant Bill Owens. But what then? Cho would know that she had known and had not told him and she knew what that would mean; he would execute her. He might even execute his own mother if he thought that she had failed to ensure that his wife had passed on all the information possible.

She knew that Cho would have no hesitation in executing her, or anybody else that he thought had either betrayed or had not supported the cause to the extent that he demanded but she couldn't let him kill her Sergeant Bill Owens. She had decided that he meant something to her; to her own surprise, she knew that he meant more to her than Cho himself.

She would not tell her mother in law of the change of date, only that her Sergeant Bill Owens was going on the patrol and that, therefore, it must be important. Perhaps Cho would never find out. She hoped not because, if Cho's men killed Sergeant Bill Owens, she would have to kill him and that meant that she would have to kill her mother in law also and she didn't want to do that; she liked the old woman.

Sergeant Owens was worried too. He was worried about the patrol, for his boys more than for himself, and he was worried that Molly had been with someone else. He had no evidence for this and, if it came to it, he had no right to deny her, but his penis itched again and he suspected that he knew what that might mean but he hoped that it didn't. "Shit!" And, he had seriously thought of marrying her and taking her back to England with him. Perhaps, if this turned out to be nothing or nothing serious, *nsu* perhaps, he would still do so; he really cared for her.

*   *   *

Challenger sailed into the bay and anchored close to the tiny One Tree Island. It had grown little since the ship had last been there. It looked like those desert islands so beloved of the writers of pirate stories; easily identifiable by the single standing tree and the treasure buried under it. It would not be possible to bury treasure or anything else on One Tree Island; with the exception of the cleft in which the cocoanut had lodged and found enough lichen and wind-blown dust to allow it to sprout, the island was solid rock. Still, it had been popular with the birds who's droppings had allowed the tree to survive.

"Special Sea Dutymen fall out. Open all X and Y openings. Hands to dinner. Up spirits." The broadcast throughout the ship lead to the inevitable response from someone of "stand fast the holy ghost" but nobody took any notice.

Ashore, the village had watched the ship enter the bay and the Headman had recognised her as the ship that had called there before. They had come in friendship, had given a jolly party for the village children and departed without causing any problems. He hoped that it would be the same this time.

He was a worried man though. If the sailors found out that the island was being used by the guerrillas, they would try to find them and then there would be a battle. He didn't want a battle. Whoever won, the village would suffer, possibly be destroyed. The sailors might even decide that the villagers should be removed from the island, for their own safety of course, and resettled in one of the new, defended villages on the mainland. He didn't want that. He liked the island and the independence that the distance from the mainland gave.

Twice, in the past year, the police boat had called at his village and twice he had convinced them that all was as it should be; no problems that need concern them. Now he would have to convince the sailors of that too and they might stay for a few days as they had last time.

Two of the fishermen's boats approached the ship, offering to sell fresh fish and as was expected, they were allowed to come alongside and show what they had for sale. In one of the boats, an English-speaking Chinese did the talking for the Malays and got them a good price for their fish.

The business concluded, the boats headed back for the beach and, in Challenger, the first lieutenant knocked on the captain's cabin door.

"Problem, Number One?"

"Not really Sir but I thought I should tell you that I'm a little surprised that one of the fishing boats that just sold us some very good fish had an English-speaking Chinese aboard."

"I take it you wouldn't be standing there if you didn't think that was important. What are you saying Number One?"

"Well Sir. When I was last here, the Headman himself came out to the ship and, to the best of my knowledge, there were no Chinese in the village. The Chinese do not as a rule take up fishing for a living and certainly there would not be just one of them, with sufficient education to speak English fluently, in a small Malay fishing village."

"Communist?"

"I suspect so Sir. Came to have a look at us and to assess the danger, I suspect."

"Then I suggest that we send you ashore, dressed in all your finery, to invite the headman aboard so that he can help us arrange a children's party as he did before. What do you think?"

"It would give me an opportunity to have a look round in the village and to get the feel of the place. If the terrorists are in control, then there will be tension in the village, eye contact will be avoided for fear of being asked questions that they don't want to have to answer."

"Are any of the islanders communists, do you think?"

"Doubt it Sir. Most of the terrorists are Chinese Chinese, sent in to stir things up. Very few of them are native to Malaya Sir, although originally of course they were all locals. These incomers live off the indigenous Chinese villagers living in the unofficial villages on the edge of the jungle.

"The locals are too scared not to give them whatever they ask for but the army have begun to sort that out. They're clearing and demolishing these unofficial villages and bringing the inhabitants in to the new, defended villages where they can be protected from the communist terrorists and the terrorists can be prevented from obtaining food etc. from the villagers.

"I understand that it is working very well and that, as a result, things are a lot better than they were a year or two ago but, of course, the communists are calling these new villages concentration camps."

"OK Harry. You get yourself sorted out and get yourself ashore with as much pomp as we can manage. We'll give the communist spy something to think about, eh? When do you think would be the earliest we could hold the party? We may not be able to hang about here for very long remember, we have that bombardment to do in a few days. We're waiting for the detailed programme but it can't be far ahead or they wouldn't have diverted us, would they."

"I'll have a word with the Chief Buffer Sir. I suspect that his boys could rig a roundabout on the capstan and a couple of swings from the gun barrels within twenty four hours; not to mention the sick bay Tiffy blowing up a box or two of French letters and painting faces on them."

"Tell the PO Chef to organise ice cream and perhaps some sticky buns or something eh? We might as well look as if we are intending only to win hearts and minds as the Americans call it."

The first lieutenant's place at the cabin door was taken by the officer of the day "All secure, Sir."

"Thank you Taffy. Have a word with Number One, will you. I rather think that he will have a few little jobs that need doing this afternoon."

"Very good Sir."

The word spread throughout the ship. There was to be a children's party on the foc'sle tomorrow afternoon. All hands would be expected to pitch in and help. A few colourful flags draped along the guardrails from the signals department, the swings to be made and fixed to the lowered gun barrel by the gunnery department and the engine room artificers were asked to help the chief bosun's mate's lads to make a roundabout and fix it to the capstan. The Chief Stoker was asked, as a favour, by the Engineer Officer to ensure that there would be sufficient steam on the capstan to give the kids a good ride.

There is nothing sailors like more than organising a children's party, with the possible exception of organising one for themselves, and all hands turned to with a will. All or almost all could remember previous parties on other ships and the fun of entertaining the kids – even if they weren't their own.

The activity aboard was observed from ashore and, when the first lieutenant in full number one dress stepped ashore from the motorboat, the village headman was standing on the beach to welcome him. The Chinese was nowhere to be seen and the first lieutenant was glad of that.

The headman recognised Lieutenant Enders from his previous visit and welcomed him in both Malay and in English.

"It is a pleasure to be here again Sir" Enders said, bowing very slightly in respect to the man's status. The gesture, though simple and cheap was appreciated by the headman, it would maintain his status in the village.

"I am very pleased to see you again Lieutenant, I am surprised that you are not by now the captain of your ship. I am sure they are waiting only for something better to offer before promoting you."

Enders smiled at him. "I am very happy to be here again and hope that all is well with your village? Is there anything that we may be able to help you with whilst we're here?"

"No, no Lieutenant. We are simple people and our demands are met, in the most part, by the island and the sea. I admit that, nowadays, we do buy paraffin and such things from the mainland, rather than relying on palm oil as our forefathers did but I am sure you would not deny us that small degree of progress."

The two men walked side by side up the beach towards the headman's house, a simple platform raised on stilts to protect the inhabitants from snakes and other wandering wildlife. The sides were open to allow the cleansing wind to remove any possible odours from the cooking that had taken place as soon as it had been seen that the officer was to come ashore. The palm frond roof kept the sun at bay and the whole was both convenient and comfortable.

They mounted the steps, the headman ushering his guest before him. "It would give me much pleasure if you would enter my house, Lieutenant."

Harry Enders knew his manners and removed his shoes at the top of the steps, before entering.

"There was no need for you to do that Lieutenant," his host said "but you honour me by following our traditions. It would be so much easier if all did so."

Enders knew that he had just been given some valuable information but knew enough not to allow that knowledge to be observable. "If, Sir, there is nothing of importance that we can do for your village, perhaps you would allow the children to come out to the ship for a party tomorrow afternoon?

"Many of the sailors are married men and fathers themselves and they would very much enjoy entertaining the children as they would their own if they were at home."

"That is most kind, Lieutenant. I remember well and with pleasure the party that your sailors gave when you last visited us and I am sure that all the children will be very happy to come out to the ship. Some of those that you entertained on your last visit are now grown and have left the island for work on the mainland but, as is the way of nature, there are just as many youngsters as ever in the village. I must remember to ask the priest how that can be."

The headman's wicked smile was returned by the first lieutenant; the older man was obviously happy to be able to show off his English and his understanding of English humour.

"I am asked by my captain to seek your permission to send a swimming party ashore. I am sure that they will cause no trouble and a picnic on dry land would be very welcome after being cooped up in the ship for so long."

"Of course Lieutenant. Please allow as many as you can spare to enjoy our hospitality. We shall provide fish for their picnic; I shall light the picnic fire myself when it grows dark."

His wife brought food and drink, setting it upon the low table in the centre of the room. She did not look at the lieutenant but he was aware that he was being observed by her. He remembered her from his last visit. She looked older now; older than she should look after only a couple of years. He looked at the chief more closely than good manners allowed but hoped that his examination would not be noticed. He too seemed to have aged more than he should have done after only a couple of years. All was not as well with the village as the headman's words would have him believe.

When politeness allowed, the first lieutenant wished his host good day and returned to the beach where the boat had waited. "Back to the ship, Cox'n but not too quickly. I think we are being observed."

"Steady does it, Sir, eh?"

"Yes please Cox'n steady does it."

He stood in the stern of the motorboat but did not look back. He was a naval officer and naval officers do not look over their shoulder to see if they are being watched.

The village headman turned from watching the boat and walked slowly back to his house. Had he said enough? Had he, perhaps, said too much? Would the lieutenant understand the delicacy of the situation here on the island? He knew that he was under observation from the fringe of the jungle and ignored it. The Chinese would be back this evening and would, no doubt, have to agree that there was no way the headman could have refused either the children's party or the beach picnic without arousing suspicion; both were traditional when naval ships visited.

"Well, Number One?"

"We were right Sir. The headman is under considerable stress from someone and he intimated that he had had visits from someone not prepared to remove his shoes when entering his house as is, as you know Sir, the custom."

"Yes, I do know Harry. I may not have been here long but I once got a badge for observation in the Boy Scouts."

"God, how long ago was that, Sir?"

"Never you mind Harry. Just bear it in mind, eh?"

"I particularly noticed that both the headman and his wife looked a great deal older than when I was last here and I suspect that he is having a lot more trouble than he would ever admit to. I imagine that the visitor refusing to remove his shoes is probably the Chinese I saw earlier, though he didn't appear to be in the village whilst I was there."

"And you think that the Chinese is the head of the terrorists?"

"I cannot be sure Sir but it would seem reasonable to assume that."

"What then? What do you suggest that I do about it?"

"Well Sir, I have arranged for the picnic ashore, the headman promised to supply fish for our supper and to light the picnic fire himself. Now that is slightly unusual, I would think. Not the fish of course but the headman lighting a picnic fire on the beach. Now I wonder why he particularly wanted to do that and also, why he particularly emphasised that he would light it when it got dark?"

"To draw attention to himself and to the beach party Harry? Was he, do you think, suggesting that whilst you and he are busy living it up on the beach, one or two carefully chosen members of the ship's company might advantageously sneak ashore further along the beach, out of the light of the fire, and take a quiet look around?"

"You could be right Sir. We could make it a rather noisy party; make sure that any watchers will be watching that rather than the other end of the beach."

"Let it be so, Number One. Now, who do we send ashore?"

"I'll sort something out Sir. We need someone with at least a semi- professional knowledge of skulduggery and a couple or more of equally qualified villains. I feel sure we can find suitable candidates Sir."

"Are you suggesting, Number One, that my ship carries villains and experts in what you so lightly describe as professional skulduggery?"

"Yes, Sir."

"Oh good. Off you go. I suppose you think it best if you don't consult me about it?"

"Yes, Sir."

"Very well."

The captain returned to his letter-writing. He would have lots to tell Sable about this trip after all. What had started out as a perfectly boring transit from Sasebo to Singapore for refit was turning into a bit of a Boy's Own Paper adventure.

TEN

Sergeant Bill Owens had given it a great deal of thought and had come to the conclusion that, patrol or no patrol, he would have to go to the sickbay and have a quiet word with the Sergeant in charge. They were friends, known each other for years and he would know what the trouble was and whether he needed to bother the quack with it.

It was one of the least sensible and most annoying rules in the army that catching a venereal disease was a punishable offence because, in order to catch it, the soldier mush have been out of bounds. All the good places were technically out of bounds but nobody much took notice of that until the dreaded VD struck and by then, it was too late to worry about the finer points of military law.

*   *   *

Molly made her way to her mother in law's house to report that her soldier had told her about the big push against the guerrillas. She told her mother in law to make sure that Cho heard about it.

"Will your sergeant go with his platoon, child?"

"Yes, mother in law. I am afraid for him."

"You are fond of this sergeant?"

"Yes mother in law but I cannot persuade him not to go. He is a soldier and soldiers must go when ordered to do so; is that not so?"

"Yes daughter it is but you should not have allowed yourself to grow fond of this Englishman, you are married to my son."

"But your son is not interested in his wife, mother in law, only in the great struggle."

"Perhaps you are right daughter but do not ever let Cho suspect that you care for this Englishman, he will surely kill him."

"I know that, mother in law and can only beg you not to tell him."

"I shall not tell him child. You may rely on me. Perhaps all will be well and your sergeant will come back and we can all carry on as before."

"I hope that that will be the way of it mother in law but I have this fear in my heart."

"I too once had such a fear, when the Japanese came and took Cho's father away to work I don't know where. I never saw him again. I hope it will not be so for you."

*   *   *

In the bay where Challenger was anchored, almost every fishing boat had been pressed into service to ferry children, and not a few of the younger parents, out to the ship. The ship's own motor boat had been dressed with flags and her crew, dressed in their best number six white uniforms, was waiting at the beach to deliver the village chief to the captain's cabin and lunch. He being a Moslem, there would be no drinks on offer but the captain was sure he too could manage without in such good cause.

Aboard Challenger, the swings had been installed on the levelled barrel of 'A' gun. Two low swings side by side and the petty officer gunner had suggested that, perhaps, they could also be used to give rides to the children by training the gun round from the starboard stop to the port stop, about two hundred and fifty degrees of travel. The gunnery officer, had instantly agreed that this was an excellent idea and that he might even, as the youngest officer on board, take such a ride himself in full uniform. It would amuse the children to see so grand a personage as the English naval officer being swung around in such a manner.

The petty officer suspected that it would amuse the ship's company too but that was no bad thing. It would show that even the youngest naval officer was, in some small degree, human also. It was, he knew, always very difficult for the young officers to maintain their dignity whilst, at the same time, behaving in the natural manner that made life on the small ships agreeable to all. There were always one or two of the hard case sailors prepared to take advantage if the opportunity arose.

Commander Powers saw his first lieutenant pass the open door of his day cabin on his way to the wardroom. "Everything laid on, Number One?"

"Yes Sir. All appears to be in hand and everyone seems to be enjoying themselves. I haven't been advised officially but I understand that King Neptune has been persuaded to visit the foc'sle during the festivities, together with his usual entourage"

"Jolly good Harry. Don't let it get too boisterous though, eh? We don't want anyone hurt or scared."

"No Sir but I imagine that one or two of the sailors may be thrown bodily over the side and a great deal of noise made in the process. Pleas for help, for mercy and all that. The kids 'll love it Sir I'm sure, they spend half their lives in the water themselves"

"So will the other sailors, I suspect. Who has been elected as volunteers for being thrown overboard, do we know?"

"I don't know Sir and, I suspect, neither do they!"

"Oh well, keep your eye on things."

The navigating officer, in his guise as the communications officer, knocked on the cabin doorpost.

"Yes Pilot?"

"I was wondering Sir, well, the yeoman was wondering, whether we might rig the dress ship overall flags for the party?"

"You don't feel that this is all getting out of hand, do you Pilot?"

"Oh no Sir. The yeoman says that it would be no trouble, that it could be rigged in about an hour."

"Might I suggest Pilot that we offer the yeoman a compromise. We don't want to upset him nor take anything from his enthusiasm but I suggest that he rigs only the for'ard section, from the Jackstaff to the mast. That will help to decorate the foc'sle and it won't be too strenuous a job to take it down again when the kids go ashore. We don't want all our men working on breaking down the party when we want them ashore having a loud and enjoyable picnic."

"Good idea Sir. I'll tell the yeoman. I imagine that that will please the signalmen."

Powers smiled at the departing young officer. He would have quite a lot to tell Sable when he got back to the letter again but that wouldn't be until after they had sailed from here or, perhaps, whilst the others were all ashore on the beach. The party was developing into quite a major operation and there had been not a single complaint that he had heard about. Everyone seemed keen to take part and to give the kids a good time. He wondered what the petty officer gunner really thought of his part in all this? He and a party of picked men were to miss the beach party; they would be landing at the far end of the beach and circling round behind the village to see what they could see.

If the island was being used on a large scale by the terrorists, either as a rest and recreation station or as a transhipment point for their smuggled arms and ammunition, then there should be a quite discernable path going into the jungle behind the village, a path that the fishermen would have had no use for.

His instructions were to find it, if it was there, and try to discern its direction. If it was possible without endangering themselves, to get even an approximate location for the terrorist's camp, a few high explosive shells delivered by another ship at a later date might cause sufficient alarm and despondency amongst its inhabitants to render the island less attractive in the future. That, at least, would help the villagers.

*   *   *

Sergeant Bill Owens stood at the door of the sick-bay, looking solemn and waiting for the results of the tests carried out the other day. His friend handed him the lab report. "Sorry mate. It ain't non-specific urethritis, its quite specific syphilis."

"Oh Shit! You absolutely sure?"

"Bill Owens. You've been in the army longer than me and you know as well as I do that *nsu* doesn't smell like that. What you have mate, is a good, old fashioned dose and you, you lucky sod, are on your way to Singapore for hospitalisation. There's a convoy going this afternoon and I'll get the major to authorise you being on it."

"But I'm to take my latest bunch of virgins on this big push on Sunday, mate. I can't just abandon 'em to the enemy's tender mercies, can I?"

"Well, just this once Bill Owens, you'll take orders not give 'em. And, you're going to hospital this afternoon. We've got it early and with this new penicillin stuff they've got in there, you'll be as right as rain in no time. Don't worry about your lads, someone else will just have to take them in hand."

"Won't the major think I'm skiving?"

"But, you ain't. And I'll tell 'im so."

Sergeant Owens went back to his barrack to pack a small bag. Where he was going, he wouldn't be needing much in the way of walking out clothing.

To tell Molly? Should he or shouldn't he? Shit, he must have got it from her so presumably she already knew but did she? She might not yet have recognised the symptoms. Well, he couldn't get out of the camp now and he would be on his way to Singapore this afternoon. It would have to wait. He would have to give some thought to Molly while down south but if he was stuck in hospital, he would have plenty of time, wouldn't he!

*   *   *

King Neptune, fully kitted out with trident, crown and bright red robe made from the largest flag B the yeoman had in the flag locker, hailed the ship from the boat to starboard of the foc'sle.

"Ahoy Challengers. I desire to come aboard your vessel. Have a suitable senior officer stand by the gangway."

The first lieutenant dutifully attended the King's arrival; the duty bosun's mate piped the 'Still' and everyone on deck stood to attention as the King climbed aboard.

"Welcome aboard, Your Majesty. How may I be of service?"

"I see a whole pack of children for'ard and I like a party. I also suspect that there may be some amongst your ship's company that have not yet been presented to me. Have any such brought to me on the foc'sle without delay."

"As you command, Your Majesty. Bosun's mate, escort His Majesty to the foc'sle and pipe for all hands not yet presented to muster forthwith."

The children stood, awe struck at King Neptune's arrival; his golden crown and bright red cloak reflected in their excited eyes.

A throne had been erected beneath the Jackstaff and King Neptune sat himself down on it, smiling at the gawping children. He beckoned the closest, the bravest, to come to him and, reaching inside his bright red cloak withdrew brightly wrapped presents for each of them.

"Come along children," he called. "King Neptune is the monarch of the deep and he has brought each and every one of you a present."

How many, if any, of the children understood him didn't matter, at the sight of the brightly wrapped gifts, all were eagerly crowding round his throne.

The gifts dispensed, the king called for the first lieutenant to attend him. "I wish all these children to be given lollywater and ice cream," he told him. "Now, where are the sailors who have not before been presented to me?"

Whilst the children were being served with diluted orange juice and ice cream, a line of about ten young sailors were assembled before the king and the ceremony began of welcoming them to King Neptune's realm. After sufficient salutation had been made to the King, the youngsters were unceremoniously thrown over the side, into the sea; much to the delight of the children many of whom followed them, diving into the water also and swimming round to the gangway ladder and climbing back onboard.

"There is just one more man, Your Majesty, who has not previously been introduced to you; the youngest officer onboard."

"Then bring him to me, I say."

Sub lieutenant Horton, in full, if not his best, uniform was brought before the king and was addressed by His Majesty.

"What's your name, boy?"

"Sub Lieutenant Horton, Your Majesty."

The children gathered round even closer. They had been amused by seeing the young sailors thrown overboard and had jumped overboard themselves to join in the fun but now there appeared a prospect that an officer, someone they could see was important, might be similarly cast overboard.

Chanting began, the sailors started it and were joined by the children who didn't understand the English words but recognised the potential meaning of the chant.

"Over he goes. Over he goes. Over he goes."

And, over he went, arms and legs flailing and crying for mercy as loudly as he could. A good swimmer, he dived down as far as he could and remained under for as long as he dared before coming back to the surface, coughing, spluttering and waving his arms about in apparent distress.

The children thought it was very funny, the sailors thought it was very funny and, secretly, the first lieutenant thought it was funny and it certainly wouldn't do the Subby any lasting harm to have his dignity thus punctured in a good cause. And he had taken it all in good part.

"Let the merriment continue," declared King Neptune, heading for the swing and demanding that he be swung both up and down and back and forth by the gun's crew peddling the manual controls in the mounting.

From the swing, he moved to the roundabout and demanded that it be rotated as quickly as was possible. The chief stoker obliged by opening the steam valve on the capstan beneath the roundabout and calling for all present to stand back.

Jelly and buns appeared from the galley and were demolished by the children happily eating things that they had never seen before but following the sailors' example with unabashed pleasure.

Below, in the for'ard messdeck, the petty officer gunner was briefing the small party that he would be leading inshore as soon as the beach party was in progress and he hoped, attracting the attention of all on shore.

"Now we are not trying to capture an enemy held island, you are not American marines looking for glory, our job is to sneak like thieves in the night behind the village and try and spot any evidence that this island is not the tropical paradise you see before you but a terrorist encampment and ammunition store. Do I make myself clear?" A general nodding of heads reassured him that he had selected the right men for the job.

"Right. As soon as this party's over and the kids have gone ashore, I want you lot to muster in the canteen flat with dark clothing, your number fours uniform is favourite and your faces and hands suitably blackened. The only white I want to see is the whites of your eyes and I don't want you showing even them to the enemy, OK?" The nodding of heads was repeated.

"There will be no guns issued but a bayonet will be issued and is to be kept well hidden unless you need to use it and, if you do need to use it, make good and sure that whoever you use it on isn't left alive to talk about it. Right, any questions?"

"What if they use guns against us, PO?"

"Then, son, you run like hell! I don't want no heroes and I don't want no dead bodies to account for when we get back onboard. The Captain has told me clear, he doesn't like writing letters to grieving wives or parents, he says he wrote enough of them in the war to last him a lifetime so watch yourselves. The first lieutenant, who we all know to be a gentleman and a scholar, has told me that there will be a double tot of neaters waiting when we get back.

"I assured him that that was not necessary, that you were all devoted subjects of the king, very probably teetotal and would lay down your lives for king and country with a light laugh but, whilst assuring me that he was certain that that was no less than he would expect me to say, he didn't believe a word of it so you gets a double tot when we gets back."

*   *   *

Sergeant Owens climbed into the back of the fifteen cwt truck and settled himself as comfortably as he could, sitting on the small suitcase in which he had packed the few belongings he thought he might need in hospital. It was a hell of a long way to Singapore and, with just one exception where it was safe to do so, the truck would not stop until it had crossed the Johor causeway onto Singapore island; extra fuel tanks had been fitted so that these long distance runs could be made without refuelling.

At his feet, his rifle and five boxes of ammunition would accompany him throughout the journey. Though there was no reason to expect the convoy to be attacked, there was no reason to doubt that, given the opportunity, the terrorists would spray it with machine gun fire as it passed along the road. Sergeant Owens remembered the advice he had given to his virgin soldiers, never stick your head out of the vehicle for a look-see, every tree looks like every other tree so it ain't worth the risk of getting it shot off and, at the first sign of any trouble, lie flat on the bottom of the truck so that the wooden side panels offer some protection.

It was the driver's job to get them out of the way of any bullets that were flying about and only if the truck stopped should they even consider getting out of it and, when they did, they should use it as protection, placing themselves behind the truck, away from the position of the enemy. The number of times he had given this advice he couldn't remember but it was sound enough for him to follow it himself should the need arise. Of course, if the first bullet killed the driver, all bets were off and it would be every man for himself.

He hadn't told Molly that he was going to Singapore and he hadn't written her a note either. If, as he must have, he had caught the infection from her then, she would very soon know about it. Nevertheless, he was sorry that she had given it to him, even if it could be cured by this new penicillin stuff the medic had told him about. Perhaps, if he could get some, he would bring some back for her to take. Annoyed as he was by her giving him the infection, he didn't like the idea of her dying of it for lack of a little medicine.

The sergeant medical orderly shook his hand. "OK? Take care of yourself mate. Don't come back here if you can avoid it eh?"

"Thanks mate. See you anon, eh? Don't get yourself killed or anything silly like that."

The medical sergeant laughed. "Don't you worry mate, I'll be right here in camp, waiting for those who get themselves shot to bring their problems to me. I ain't going out there looking for trouble, I'm too bloody old for all that now. See you in the bar, somewhere, OK?"

The convoy passed through the gate and Sergeant Owens looked towards the town of Terengganu. "So long Mol, love. It was fun while it lasted."

ELEVEN

The children's party had been a great success, particularly the fully bearded and enrobed King Neptune. Now the darkness closed around the small group on the beach, hiding them from the larger, noisier group surrounding the big fire some hundred yards away.

"Right, no talking and no unnecessary noise."

The Petty Officer lead the small group of darkly-dressed men with their faces and hands blacked, into the primary jungle behind the beach. There was no path here, any normal foot traffic would have used the beach but the undergrowth was sparse enough to allow them relatively untroubled passage whilst providing sufficient cover to prevent them being seen by anyone watching.

This was not the first time that Petty Officer Mervin Little had led or been a member of such a group. As the ship's gunnery instructor and un-armed and close combat expert, he was the best man to send away ashore with or without a gun and he knew exactly with whom else onboard he would risk his life.

Leading Seaman Geof Booker was no longer a young man by naval standards, he had three good conduct stripes on the sleeve of his uniform and had joined the navy as a boy of fifteen seventeen years ago. He should long since have been promoted but he didn't want to be. He preferred the Leading rate; maximum pay with minimum responsibility, he told anyone who asked.

Able Seaman Masters was another old timer though he currently had only two good conduct stripes, having forfeited the third for some insubordination almost a year ago. He would get it back by the end of the year, he knew that and meanwhile, he was comfortable in the knowledge that, as far as his messmates were concerned, he still had his third badge.

As captain of 'B' gun, he was well known to and trusted by Petty Officer Little. What the able seaman chose to do when ashore was none of Petty Officer Little's business but when involved with guns, Able Seaman Masters was entirely reliable and even if, as tonight, the gun had been replaced by a bayonet only, he had no hesitation in trusting him to watch his back. Able Seamen Bob Andrews, Colin Baker, and Sam Bennett, chosen for their reliability and steadfastness when challenged, made up the party.

The light from the fire cast long shadows across the beach and into the first few feet of the undergrowth beneath the outward-leaning palm trees and ensured that anyone watching would have his night vision ruined. They were safe for the moment. Out in the bay, the anchored Challenger lay illuminated by the moonlight; everything was as they wanted it, quiet, normal and unthreatening. What Little wanted, more than anything else, was that they should complete their reconnaissance without being seen or heard; certainly without being challenged.

Behind the village, they found the track leading to the small plantations of vegetables that the fishermen grew; what they were looking for was a well-defined path from these small gardens further into the jungle. That would indicate that someone, quite a lot of someones, were in the habit of passing through the village, the gardens and deeper into the jungle; something that the fishermen would have no reason to do. Even in the dark, with only the light of a young moon to help them, they had no difficulty in finding just such a path.

There had been no attempt to hide it. Whoever had made it was not concerned that others might see it and recognise it for what it was. The fishermen and their families all knew about the path and the camp to which it led and could be relied upon not to interfere with the passing of the almost exclusively Chinese visitors who passed along it. There had been one of the elders in the village who had objected to the so-called freedom fighters using their island but he had disappeared one night and the rest of the villagers had never enquired about his going.

Petty Officer Little waved his party down. "Right, we've found the path we're looking for. Now we see where it goes. If I was running the camp that I think is at the end of this path, I would have posted sentries at about this point, just to check who was cheeky enough to come along it.

"Charlie Masters, take point to port, I don't want to be surprised by a whole herd of Chinese coming down that path from their camp, OK?"

"OK PO but don't sneak up behind me and stick it up me by mistake, eh"

Masters disappeared into the trees on the left of the path without a sound. Remarkable, thought Little, how quietly seamen could move when they didn't want to be heard, even on shore. Once off the cleared path, the long grass cover thinned to extinction where no sun could reach the ground.

After a few minutes' wait to let him get far enough ahead of them and to flush out anyone hiding on that side of the path, Able Seaman Andrews disappeared into the trees on the right hand side with a similar intent. The rest of the party kept silent for a few more minutes then slowly followed the path.

The path led through the trees, wide enough spaced to open up a source of sunlight during the day and, luckily, the moon tonight. The daytime sunlight had allowed tall grass to grow at either side of the path and it was into this that the four men slipped when a faint sound was heard from ahead.

There it was again. A scurrying sound, almost as if some animal disturbed by the men who had gone ahead was running for cover, but that couldn't be right; the sound was coming towards them. Peering through the long grass Petty Officer Little saw a stone bounce twice then roll to the side of the path.

Stones didn't move about on their own initiative, even a sailor knew that. The men waited.

A moment later, four men came down the path. The first carried an AK47 automatic rifle and the second a sack. Behind them, rifles hanging over their shoulders, the other two carried what appeared to be half a tree trunk.

The crouching sailors let them pass and waited a few moments longer, to see if any more would follow. There was just the suggestion of a sound, enough to warn them without alarming the four that had gone on down the path.

Masters and Andrews showed themselves for a moment before moving into the long grass beside the Petty Officer.

"What do you reckon PO? Where do you suppose they're going?"

"Well, with that log, they could just be going to our party on the beach and I don't fancy the chances of our lot if they open fire with them AK's at close range."

"What do you reckon we should do about it then?"

"Well we know the camp must be a little further up this path so we can come back later if we need to. In the meantime, I think we'd better take a closer look at that little lot."

They fell into line some distance behind the Chinese and followed them towards the beach where the noise of the beach party would cover any sound that they might be making.

Close to the village, they could hear the party's laughter and chatter and could see the silhouette of the four Chinese against the moonlit sea.

"They ain't after the beach party then PO."

"No Charley they ain't."

"What then?"

"We watch."

They hunkered down, hidden below one of the village houses. The Chinese, almost invisible in their black, loose fitting pyjama suits of jacket and trousers, appeared to be holding some sort of conference on the foreshore, hidden from the people on the beach but in view, silhouetted against the sea, to those under the house.

Satisfied that they had not been seen or heard by the revellers, two of the men carried the tree trunk down to the water and came back for the sack.

"Christ! PO, they're after the ship. They must have a bomb or something in that sack."

"Right, Masters, you and I will take out the two still carrying guns. You three, I want the others dead and the sack back here before anyone sees or hears anything, OK?"

Unaware that they were themselves now the hunted rather than the hunters, the two Chinese moved down the beach and into the water, pushing the tree trunk before them for support. The others, watching them from the edge of the village, heard nothing as Petty Officer Little and Able Seaman Masters slipped out from under the house and into the sparse undergrowth. It was done in a moment. The left hand round from behind and clasped over the mouth to prevent a cry and the right hand thrusting the bayonet almost vertically upwards from just to the left of the spine, through the lung and into the heart in a single movement. They held the weight for a moment, allowing the men to die, before lowering them silently to the ground.

In the water, eyes fixed on the ship to seaward, the two terrorists pushed the log before them, under which was suspended the sack. Quiet as they were, they made sufficient noise to prevent them hearing the three swimmers coming up and overtaking from behind.

The sailors trod water for a moment, resting. Bob Andrews tapped the other two on the shoulder to attract their attention. He tapped Colin Baker once more and pointed to the right hand swimmer ahead and pointed Sam Bennett towards the other. He indicated by sign that he would go underneath them and grab the sack and the log.

Swimming under water, he could see the log above him, the sack hanging down from it. Behind the log, he could see the two Chinese paddling noisily, pushing the log towards the ship.

He glanced behind him and could see the others closing on the Chinese swimmers. He placed himself in position to grab the sack just as the two Chinese simultaneously let go of the log and disappeared downwards, leaving a red stain above them. With hardly a ripple, Able Seamen Baker and Bennett surfaced, grinning at each other. Andrews, hanging on to the log, pointed towards the beach. "Go," he told them, "never mind grinning at each other like the idiots you are."

"Like taking sweeties from kids, PO."

"If you ever take sweeties from kids like that, Able Seaman Bennett, I will personally take them from you in a similar manner, OK?"

"Just a manner of speaking PO, I wouldn't do anything like that for real."

The beach and their breath regained, they opened the sack.

"Right Andrews. Let's have ourselves a look-see into the sack, shall we? See what we've caught."

Two heavy limpet mines spilled onto the ground; the Chinese hieroglyphics clearly identifying their country of origin. "Fuck me PO, those buggers would have taken out half of the ship's side. What we going to do with them?"

"For the moment, nothing. I want to go back up that path and see what else they have that might be interesting. Leading Seaman Booker, you wash yourself, look like a partygoer and slip along to the beach party and tell the Jimmy what's happened, tell him the rest of us will be back well before daybreak or not at all, OK?"

"Don't make jokes like that PO, they have a habit of coming true."

"Oh, and you might just mention that there's a couple of dead bodies here that wants to be removed from the scene of the crime as you might say. Don't want the villagers upset, do we."

Once again they crept up the path, Able Seaman Bennett taking the lead. He stopped when he could see the first of the huts in front of him.

From the path, the camp looked asleep. As far as they could see, there were no guards, indeed, there being no perimeter fencing of any kind, there would have been no point in placing a guard anywhere other than perhaps at the end of the path. From where they were hidden, there appeared no signs of life except for a single dim light in one of the huts.

"What do you reckon PO?"

"Nice spot for a quiet holiday, I should say. Not what you'd call a lot of fun but I expect they just want a nice quiet week off work. Could do with something like that myself."

The huts, really just raised platforms with roofs and palm frond sides which could be raised during the day to increase ventilation, miniature versions of the village houses, were placed between the trees. There was no large, central open space, just a relatively small trodden area too small to attract attention by over-flying aircraft.

"Do we go in?"

"Quietly! we don't want to wake anyone up, do we?"

Bennett pointed towards the hut with the light showing.

"What do you reckon PO? That the headquarters hut and someone waiting up for his lads to get back and report success?"

"If his lads had been successful, he'd have expected them back about now, even if the mines had been set for maximum timing, they should go off any time about now. No. If there's anyone awake in there, he's wondering what the hell's gone wrong and that means that he's wide awake and worried."

"How many do you reckon there might be here PO?"

"What's on your mind Charlie?"

"I was just thinking that, as we now have their guns and their mines, we could do a certain amount of damage if we stuck one under a couple of the huts and torched the rest. We could shoot anyone who come out of 'em."

"We could certainly cause mayhem, mate. That's for certain but I don't think the Captain wants us starting world war three while half his ship's company are lying on the beach, pissed."

"But PO, what if they came out of the huts and we had to defend ourselves. He wouldn't mind so much then, would he?"

"Charlie Andrews, you're a devious bastard but you could be right."

The clockwork timers on the limpet mines were wound up to allow just five minutes before they exploded, the mines were placed under the hut with the light showing and under the bigger one next to it. There was no way of discovering whether that belonged to the camp commander or was some sort of store but, either way, its destruction couldn't do the camp any good.

Handfuls of dried grass were pulled and stacked around the legs of the hut platforms and anything else that they could find that was dry and burnable was added and lit.

"Right, I want one of you on each side of the camp and remember to fire into the camp, not right across it into each other, OK? Pick a target and kill it, don't just spray bullets all over the bloody island, we haven't got enough for that. Right, off you go; you've got about a minute before all hell breaks loose. And, for God's sake keep your heads down, you know how the Captain hates writing letters to the wives and parents of deceased sailors."

The two bombs went off almost simultaneously, engulfing the smaller of the two mined huts in flame and debris. The other hut had obviously been the magazine and the explosion must have been heard on the beach.

Bodies, in various stages of undress, fell out of the huts that had been set on fire, none of them carrying a weapon. The concerted fire from the jungle on all four sides of the camp and no doubt some of their own ammunition exploding in the fiercely burning magazine hut claimed twenty- four Chinese and three Tamils before Petty Officer Little shouted for them to cease fire and make for the path, out of the way of any more exploding ammunition.

They waited. No more terrorists came out of the huts and the ammunition hut fire had burned down to a heap of glowing embers, lying silently radiating a fierce heat but no sound.

The sailors gathered in the centre of the camp to see what damage they had done.

"What's these blacks doing here PO?"

"They ain't blacks son, them's Tamils, Indian workers imported by the rubber planters 'cos the Chinese is too clever to do tapping and the Malays is too lazy. There's a few of 'em joined up with the terrorists during the war when the Japs was worse than the Brits had been."

A single shot from beneath one of the still burning huts hit Colin Baker in the left buttock. He turned and let rip with the AK at his assailant.

"I've been hit PO. Some bastard's shot me up the arse!"

"Well, at least we can claim that he was chasing you and the rest of us had to open fire to save your other buttock from damage."

"It ain't bloody funny Mervin Little! It's fucking painful."

"OK son, we'll carry you back as a true hero, a casualty of war. You never know son, you might get sent home with a medal."

"With my luck, I'll end up in the sick bay in HMS Terror in Singers and get all the sympathy that the navy always hands out."

"That's the spirit, lad. Take it on the chin or, in this case, up the arse."

They were still laughing at Baker's misfortune when they walked out of the trees on to the beach.

TWELVE

From his day cabin porthole, Commander Powers could see the fire on the beach and the people gathered round it. It was too far to hear anything but, from what he could see, it was safe to assume that a good time was being had by all. Aboard, all was now quiet.

'My Darling.' He read what he had written previously and carried on writing. 'We are anchored in the big bay at Redang island where we had hoped to trap and capture a junk bringing arms and ammunition to the terrorists but she escaped us. Rather than waste our trip here, we have had a children's party this afternoon for the islanders' children who had a great time and, I suspect, so did the sailors.

'There were swings suspended from the barrel of 'A' gun and a roundabout mounted on the capstan. King Neptune paid us a visit and initiated a couple of the younger sailors (who I suspect had been initiated previously but didn't want to spoil the fun for the kids) and Neptune's helpers threw young Paul Horton, the gunnery officer, over the side fully dressed. I hope he has another uniform for Sunday Divisions.

'The Sick Bay provided a gross or so of condoms which the sailors inflated and drew faces on and every child went home full of ice cream, buns and carrying their own 'balloon'.

'Tonight, I can see them all, the sailors that is, on the beach having a bonfire party and no doubt surreptitiously drinking some of the local screech brewed by the islanders for their own use. Harry Enders is ashore with them and as long as he doesn't tell me about it I shan't know. I can only hope that not too many are hung over in the morning when we must leave here.

'I suspect that the junk is hanging about somewhere out of sight, waiting for an opportunity to come in and unload. The islanders, Malay fishermen and their families, are not terrorists nor, I don't think, are they even sympathisers with the communists but they are few, they are family men and they are in no position to do much about the terrorists who have set up a holiday camp in the jungle with which most of the island is covered.

'We know about it of course and will do something about it at some stage but at the moment it is more important to trap and sort out the supply junk than to interrupt the holiday of a few tired and probably disenchanted terrorists. Funny really, we use a similar island further south as a rest and recreation centre for our own soldiers who are withdrawn from the jungle on rotation.

'Just to be sure that they are not hatching anything too dangerous, we have sent a small patrol into the jungle to spy out their camp and to assess the numbers present. On the whole, it is the opinion of those above us that the camp is less trouble here where we can keep an eye on it than buried somewhere else in the jungle on the mainland where we can't.

'In one respect, the beach party is a cover for the more covert operation going on behind the beach but we would probably have had one anyway, it's good PR and as the Yanks keep telling us, we have to win over the hearts and minds of the natives.

'As we have been trying to ready suitably qualified Malays for independence since before the war, although the Japanese occupation slowed things down a bit, I don't think the Yanks can teach us much about local politics.

'Well, Darling, we're off in the morning and hope to catch up with our suspect junk but even if we don't, we have another little excitement in view. 'It seems that we are required to give some heavy gun support to a major push ashore on the mainland by the army now that the weather is better.

'There is, we are advised, a major terrorist encampment in a valley about five miles inland and with our guns' range of about twice that on a good day, we have been asked to do a little scare 'em and flush 'em bombardment. It seems that the army don't want us to actually bombard the camp, rather to overshoot so that the occupants will either stay put or move towards the soldiers approaching from the coast. Devious beggars, these army types, you know!'

A knock on the open door's post warned of the steward's approach with coffee. "Thought you might appreciate this, Sir. The wardroom stewards are packing up now as there's only the Officer of the Day onboard and I thought I'd steal this before they threw it away."

"Thank you, that's very thoughtful. I imagine the others will be back on board in the early hours or whenever the booze runs out, whichever is the sooner, eh?"

The explosion was heard quite clearly although it was far enough away to have no effect on the ship. The captain and his steward looked at each other in silence.

"Shit! What was that?"

"I know what it was Masters, the question is why was it? Ask the Officer of the Day to come in will you?"

Lieutenant Darling, the Officer of the Day, knocked on the doorpost and entered. "I heard the explosion and the Quartermaster is sure he saw it well inland from the beach so it may not mean that our people are under attack but I have turned out the duty watch. If you think it wise, Sir, we could arm them and send them ashore to protect the unarmed partygoers. Get them back to the ship as quickly as possible. "

"I think that's very wise Pilot. Perhaps you'd better go with them; I'll stand guard, as it were. Get them back as quickly as you can. Tow the whaler inshore and load that up too. Oh, and I want the first lieutenant back here in the first boat; understood?"

"Aye aye, Sir."

The explosion was even louder to those partying on the beach and suddenly all the fun seemed to go out of the party.

"Christ! What was that?"

The first lieutenant looked at the gunnery officer, who had asked what had to be the silliest question of the evening. "That, Guns, was a bloody great explosion and I suspect that I know what it was. Get the men spread out so that they present a lot of small targets rather than one bloody great mob will you, just in case we come under fire. Have the signalman call up the ship and ask them to send the boats in to collect everybody, will you.

"Taffy," he turned to Lieutenant Evans, "I think you and I might usefully wander along to the village and make enquiries whether they are responsible for this interruption of our festivities although I doubt it very much. I'm reasonably certain that it will have been our own foraging party that we sent inland, but why they have done that I just don't know. I hope it doesn't cause too much trouble for everybody else.

"Chas, Lieutenant Turner. Get these guys sorted out into some semblance of defence positions, digging themselves into the sand might be a good start, don't want them presenting too good a target if we've upset somebody. Come along Taff, let's be about it."

The village was alive with interest, lights burning in every house and villagers gathering on the beach.

"Hallo Chief. Was that anything to do with you?"

The village headman shook his head. "No Sir, I thought it might be something to do with you."

"Not directly Sir. We do have a foraging party inland, taking a look-see at what your guests are up to but they have no orders to create an embarrassing situation. Their job was to spy out what the enemy were doing and how many were doing it. Nothing more. I hope that we haven't inadvertently created a difficult situation for you."

Petty Officer Little appeared at the trot from the jungle behind the village. "Sorry about that, Sir. A little misunderstanding, you might say. We was taking a look-see at the camp as the captain asked us to when someone shot young Baker Sir.

"As we had the guns and mines we had taken off of the swimmers what you know about Sir, we returned their fire and lobbed the limpet mines under a couple of the biggest huts."

"And?"

"Well, Sir, them being mostly asleep when the shooting started, we sort of had the advantage and shot 'em as they came tumbling out of their huts. Sir."

"What? All of them?"

"Well, yes Sir. I'm afraid so. Should we have kept one for you Sir?"

"Don't push your luck Petty Officer Little. You're probably in enough trouble as it is."

"No Sir. Yes Sir. As you say Sir."

"Tell me Petty Officer. Just how many was all of them?"

"About thirty, Sir. 'course, one or two might have scapa'd into the jungle but I don't think so. We counted twenty-hour Chinese and four Tamils and, with the four we got earlier, Sir, that makes a nice round number."

"I'm not convinced that it's being a nice round number necessarily means that you got all of them but, if you think it's safe to stand up, perhaps you would help get as many of the men as possible into the boats and take charge of the rest until the boats can come back for them."

"Aye aye Sir."

"Oh, and Petty Officer Little, you had better have a better explanation ready for when you get back on board. The captain is going to want to know exactly what happened and he will want to believe it if he's going to include it in his report of this event."

"Yes, Sir. I'll give it some thought."

As the petty officer disappeared into the darkness along the beach, the navigating officer took his place. "First Lieutenant Sir. Captain would be grateful if you would go back to the ship with the first boat. I think he wants some sort of explanation Sir."

"Thank you Pilot. Get as many as you can into the boats, I'll be along in a moment."

He turned to the village headman. "Sorry about this, Sir. Would you like me to leave a few armed men here ashore to protect the village. Just in case there are some terrorists left?"

"No, thank you. I think perhaps it would be best if you and your sailors were gone by the morning so that we can deny all knowledge of whatever happened tonight. If there are any of the communists left out there, they will want to hurt somebody and it would be better if you weren't here when they come to the village. If there are any left, we shall deal with them ourselves and it would be very much better for everybody if you didn't know about it."

"I understand Sir. Well, sorry, again. That wasn't part of the plan, I assure you. We wanted the junk bringing the supplies but now they have nobody to give them to so we may get lucky after all. Goodbye. Perhaps, one day soon we can meet again in time of peace."

"I hope so Lieutenant. I do hope so."

They shook hands and Lieutenant Enders walked down to the boats. "Right Cox'n, off we go, eh?"

He glanced behind him as the boat drew away from the shore. There were still more men ashore than in the boats and it would take some time to get them all back onboard. He silently rehearsed what he would say to the captain who had, quite specifically, stated that he didn't want any trouble ashore; not from the foraging patrol nor from the beach party. Ah well, if I can't take a joke, I shouldn't have joined.

THIRTEEN

'My Darling.' Whilst waiting for the boats to return and for the first lieutenant, the captain returned to his letter. 'My Darling, all hell seems to have broken loose ashore; a couple of explosions and some gun fire. I do hope it sounds worse than it is!

'As none of the men ashore at the beach party is armed, it can only be the terrorists who have decided to attack them; a most unexpected development as they tend to want to pretend that they're not even on the island. I dread to think what might have happened. The boat's crews I have sent in to collect my men are armed of course but they would be no match for a determined enemy.'

The knock on the doorpost announced the arrival of Petty Officer Masters, a large gin and tonic in one hand and a sandwich on a plate in the other. "Thought it might be a long night, Sir."

"Thank you, I think you had better rouse out the other stewards, the rest of the officers are on their way back and will probably want something, a large amount of strong black coffee would be a good idea."

"Done that, Sir."

"Well done."

His place was taken at the cabin door by the first lieutenant, cap in hand.

"Well Harry What happened? I can't hear any shooting so presumably whatever it was is now over."

"Not as bad as it sounded actually, Sir. First of all, our patrol met one of theirs coming the other way. Four men armed, carrying a couple of limpet mines in a sack and a large log.

"Petty Officer Little let them pass and then followed them down to the beach. It became obvious that two of them were going to swim out to the ship with the sack suspended from the log so Little very properly took the action he thought appropriate."

"And what was that?"

"He and Leading Seaman Booker collar'd the two terrorists still at the top of the beach and the others followed the two Chinese swimmers into the water. Unencumbered, they were able to take out the two terrorists and recover both the log and the sack."

Petty Officer Masters appeared at the cabin door again with two cups of coffee on a tray. "Thought the first lieutenant would appreciate this, Sir."

"Thank you Masters, put it down on the table will you. Now, Harry, what was all the banging and shooting I heard?"

"As his party had removed the danger to the ship and were now armed with the terrorists' guns and also the two limpet mines in the sack, he decided to return to the camp and spy out the situation as originally ordered; sending leading Seaman Booker to report to me on the beach.

"As I could not easily recall him, I thought the best course was to continue with our loud merrymaking on the beach so that anyone watching us would not know that the patrol were in the jungle behind them."

"Yes, I see. I would probably have done the same thing but I would have tried to get a message back to the ship just in case there was a second attack group; we could have prepared a welcome for them. However, you didn't and fortunately, there wasn't. Well, what happened then?"

"Not entirely clear at the moment Sir. The patrol turned up on the beach with apparently one casualty, Able Seaman Baker, and as I was instructed to come off with the first boat, I brought them off with me. Able Seaman Baker is in sickbay having a bullet removed from his bottom and the rest of the patrol is outside Sir. I thought it might save time if Petty Officer Little reported directly to you."

"Well, he should have had time by now to have developed an explanation for why he started a fire fight when explicitly ordered to sneak about but not disturb anybody. I imagine Able Seaman Baker is none too happy about it either. Get Petty Officer Little in here then and you'd better stay so that we all know what the situation is. So far this secret mission has managed to lose the junk we were supposed to capture and wake up a whole camp full of terrorists that we were supposed to locate but not disturb; that's the army's prerogative. I suspect I shall have to explain all this to the CinC in due course."

"I'll get him in, Sir."

Petty Officer Little was a long-service rating and by virtue of his rank had no fear of being questioned. He had also, in the sixteen years he had been in the service, learned how to present a case before an officer.

"Well, Petty Officer Little, what can you tell me about this shambles? I gather that first you killed four terrorists and relieved them of not only their guns but also a couple of limpet mines that were intended for the ship. For that, at least, I must thank you and therefore presumably forgive you the sin of murder. What happened next?"

"Well Sir, having saved the ship....."

"Don't push your luck Little, you're safe and dry so far but have a care; this was supposed to be a silent, spying mission not world war three!"

"Yes, Sir. Well, once the ship was safe, I decided to return to the original order to find and examine their camp. When we had done that and we was creeping away quietly like, one of 'em wakes up and shoots Able Seaman Baker in the arse, sorry Sir, his bottom. Luckily we had the captured guns so we returned the fire and killed 'em all. There seemed no point in leaving the camp intact so we set the bombs under the two largest huts which we assumed to be the officers' quarters and torched the rest. I'm afraid we was wrong in that assumption Sir. The biggest hut must have been their ammunition store 'cos it went up like November the fifth.

"I like your version of the evening's events Petty Officer Little and that, with one or two grammatical amendments, is what I shall tell the CinC. We can only hope that he doesn't hear from some other source that the explosions preceded the shooting; that might suggest to a suspicious mind that the engagement was not quite as described and that your party saw an opportunity to destroy the camp and, hopefully, its campers and took it in direct contravention of your explicit orders. That would not only reflect badly on your hitherto unblemished record of service but also upon my chances of further promotion; I wouldn't like that."

"But Sir, we only shot back after Baker was hit Sir."

"Good man Little. You stick to that story and we might both come out of this with a thank you note from the army. Carry on.

"What do you think Harry? Was any of that true?"

"At a guess Sir, I would say that about ninety five percent was gospel but he might have got his continuity a little mixed up."

"Good. Ninety five percent must be almost a record for post-action reports. We'll go with that then, shall we?"

"Very wise, Sir."

"Right Harry. I think we had better maintain the watch on deck in case the gallant petty officer miscalculated his total kill and we'll sail at 0800. Can I leave the arrangements to you?"

"Of course Sir. I'll speak to the Chief, make sure that the engineroom department is on top line."

*   *   *

Petty Officer Little gathered the uninjured members of his patrol on the quarterdeck, well out of earshot of everybody else.

"Right. This is our story. We was creeping away from the camp when we was spotted and young Baker got shot in the arse. Well, we couldn't let 'em get away with that so we returned fire. We was very lucky that we was all wide awake and most of them was still half asleep so we got all of the bastards.

"No ifs, no buts, that's the story I've told the captain and that's the story he's going to give to the CinC. So, watch your tongues OK? Now, get your heads down, we're sailing at 0800."

*　　　*　　　*

The coffee had gone cold and he pushed it to one side, wondering whether he should add the explanation of the evening's events to his letter. He drew the paper towards him, it would help him formulate the report he would send to the CinC in the morning; that would have to be as accurate as possible and still be entirely believable. He started writing.

'So, my Love, that's what happened and, if we can find the junk and carry out our bombardment without killing too many of our own soldiers, we may yet come out of this looking better than we deserve.'

He placed the letter in its drawer and turned off the desk light. He was tired and his night cabin beckoned. Petty Officer Masters was still in his pantry. "Coffee at half past six. OK?"

"Right Sir. Good night."

"Good night."

*　　　*　　　*

Sixty miles away, off Kota Bharu, the junk Flying Tiger lay anchored, close inshore, hidden by the background clutter from any police or naval patrol ship's radar.

Lieutenant Wo lay on his bunk, satisfied that he had escaped whoever had been waiting for him at the island but worried that someone had been waiting. Clearly he had been expected and whatever was waiting was not some small police patrol boat. The sky explosion was, he suspected, a star shell that had failed to drop its flare and that meant that it was navy and that in turn meant that the small boat he had seen on his radar was probably manned by a fully armed boarding party. He had had a lucky escape.

Sleep wouldn't come. His nerves were wound up like a two-dollar watch.

He turned onto his back, looking up at the deckhead above him, wide awake. He couldn't contact his base by radio, his instructions were clear about that. The radio, secreted under the toilet bowl, was for receiving instructions only and was to be used only at the arranged transmission times. Any transmission he could make in an emergency could not be responded to in time to be of any assistance and would certainly be monitored by the British who would then know not only that the junk was there but also the frequency on which signals were transmitted, thus exposing them to the British listeners who would have no trouble translating them.

Unable to sleep, he rose and went on deck where the moon provided just enough light to walk back and forth without actually tripping over something.

Odd, he thought. If the authorities knew that he was coming then why all the theatricals of star shells and boarding parties? They had only to wait until he had anchored and then place a motor launch against each side of his ship; that would have been sufficient, it didn't need big ships with big guns.

Perhaps he was wrong. Perhaps they didn't know who he was, what sort of ship would be making the delivery, only that a delivery was expected. That made sense.

In that case, they might use a warship to illuminate any vessel approaching so that it could be identified before any attempt to arrest it. If he had been a Chinese naval vessel, they would have to decide whether an attempt to board and arrest was worth the political fall-out; he had been well outside the territorial limit when the shell had exploded and, whatever his nationality, perfectly entitled to be there.

Unfortunately, once he had increased to twenty-four knots, they would have known he was a hostile and if they had had enough light to see him, then his cover as a junk was blown. In that case, they would in future stop and search every junk; he would just have to wait and see.

Half satisfied that this was the explanation, he turned aft again to return to his bunk. Far to the south a sudden flash of bright light lit up the night sky, slowly dying away. It looked like another star shell but, if that was the case, they had not recognised him as an enemy vessel, perhaps just a smuggler, so had waited to illuminate the next target that their radar detected approaching the island.

He liked that explanation. It fitted all the facts and it meant that he was still safe from suspicion. His high speed departure was, he accepted, suspicious but it in no way detracted from his being a smuggler. He looked again towards where the flash had been but there was nothing to be seen. If the British warship was still there, waiting for him to make his delivery, he would disappoint them by landing his cargo here in Kota Baru. Those ashore would just have to organise the onward delivery to the jungle camp. At worst, the attacks on the villages and plantations would be delayed for a few days; a week perhaps but at least they would receive the arms and ammunition they needed.

He continued walking his deck, undecided whether to turn in and not sleep or stay on deck and be tired in the morning, when he would go ashore at Kota Bahru and make arrangements for his cargo to be collected and taken ashore. He was going to be tired in the morning anyway, he thought, so he lit another cigarette and collected the bottle of good Scotch whisky that he kept in the drawer under his bunk. Better than the Chinese equivalent!

He sat down on a coil of rope, allowing his bottom to fit snugly into the empty space in the centre. It was a fine, cool night and by the third swig from the bottle, sleep claimed him.

FOURTEEN

Sergeant Owens' platoon was not happy. Sergeant Owens had trained them well, they were now what the Colonel called jungle-ready, but without Sergeant Owens they were less sure of themselves than perhaps they needed to be. Sergeant Smith, Owens' replacement, was a perfectly competent NCO but it wasn't the same. He hadn't trained them so he didn't trust them and because he hadn't trained them, they didn't trust him.

The lieutenant inspected them standing rigidly to attention on the parade ground, checking that each was properly dressed and that all the equipment that they would be required to carry with them into the jungle was both present and in good order.

"Sergeant Smith. All seems to be in order. You may dismiss the men. As I understand it, the patrol will embus at zero six hundred tomorrow morning; make sure that they are ready."

"Sir."

The lieutenant walked away, back towards the mess and a cup of tea. He was worried. This was to be a major operation, every available man was to be involved and, with the terrorists in front of them and the navy shooting over their heads, there was every possibility of someone getting hurt. It was a safe bet that, despite all the secrecy, someone had given the game away and that the terrorists would be expecting them.

Hopefully, the terrorists wouldn't know precisely when the attack would take place nor from what direction but they would almost certainly be on their guard. His men would have to assume that this was so, even if in fact they were lucky and their attack came as a complete surprise to the enemy.

They had done what they could to ensure surprise by bringing forward the attack by three days. Pity about Sergeant Owens being on the sick list though, both he and the platoon would have felt happier with that old soldier in their group. Silly bugger getting syphilis; should have known better.

The lieutenant hadn't yet decided whether to put Owens on a charge as a result of picking up the infection. He must have been out of bounds to meet the woman from whom he got it and that was technically an offence. He would think about it. If he lived through the coming engagement he might give the matter some more thought; God knows, the infection should be punishment enough. Owens was a good soldier and the army needed good soldiers. He hoped this new penicillin stuff worked as well as was claimed. He would feel safer as well as happier when Owens was returned to duty.

The steward brought him his cup of tea. The trucks would take them out of the camp, looking as much like a normal convoy as possible, and head towards the KL road as if they were on their way down south. Once out of sight of any likely observers, the last-in-line lorry had been instructed to suffer a breakdown and block the road behind them so that they couldn't be followed and their disembarkation point noted.

Once they were close enough to the estimated position of the terrorist's camp, a Lysander spotter plane would over-fly the area and would report the fall of shot from the naval bombardment. The idea was that the navy's high explosive shells should impact about a quarter of a mile to the west of the encampment, on the other side of the river and thus hopefully encouraging the terrorists to either remain where they were or to retreat to the east, towards the oncoming soldiers. He remembered Sergeant Owens' favourite expression at times like this. "If you believe in God, Sir, this might be a good time to pray."

He was not absolutely sure that he did believe but was prepared to take Sergeant Owens' other piece of free advice onboard. "Even if you don't believe, Sir, a short, carefully worded prayer might not be entirely wasted."

*   *   *

HMS Challenger lay close inshore just to the south of Terengganu. Five miles inland, due west from their position, was a large lake and on one of the small rivers feeding this lake, the terrorist encampment had been long established and well hidden from the air. Unlike the British army, which liked orderly encampments with a central parade ground and roads between the major buildings, the terrorists preferred to distribute their palm frond roofed huts amongst the trees and ensure that no large open spaces were observable from above. The only truly open areas were those in which they grew their vegetables and these were many, small and hopefully invisible from the air.

"What's the time Pilot?"

"O seven three O, Sir. Half an hour should do it. We should hear from the spotter plane that he's in position any minute now."

Commander Powers spoke into the telephone to the Director above him.

"Right, Guns, is everything ready?"

"Yes, Sir. All guns loaded with HE, should make quite an impression when the first salvo lands. I wouldn't want to be on the receiving end."

"Well, Guns, you won't be today anyway. They have nothing they can shoot back at us with. This isn't like Korea where they were able to not only return our fire but often, outgun us, eh?"

"No Sir. We should be grateful for that, I suppose."

"Just think how the army feels with the terrorists in front of them and us behind them. I imagine there are quite a few of them offering up a short prayer that we don't undershoot by mistake."

"Rather them than me, Sir."

Standing by the RT receiver with his earphones on, one earpiece twisted up away from his ear so that he could hear what was going on on the bridge as well as any message coming over the radio, Yeoman Houser listened to this conversation with some amusement.

He had heard the same or a very similar conversation immediately prior to just about every bombardment the ship had done off the coast of Korea. It was a kind of ritual, the jocular attitude allowed them to blank out of their minds the inevitable death and destruction that must ensue. None of the men in Challenger, nor in any other ship in which he had served, was intrinsically wicked, none of them actually wanted to kill or maim anyone but this was a warship and that was what happened in a war.

"Spotter plane says he's in position Sir. We can open fire as convenient."

"Decent of him. OK Guns, let's be having you. We'll wait for fall of shot reports before the second salvo."

"Very good Sir."

The guns had been following the target for the last quarter of an hour or, more accurately, the guns had remained pointing at the target as the ship moved slowly between the two points on the chart that limited their area of action.

"Main armament only, one round high explosive, Shoot, Shoot, Shoot."

The firing gongs dinged an instant before each gun fired and those on the bridge heard only two dings, so close together were the firings from the four 4.5 inch mountings

"All guns, high explosive, load, load, load."

The recoil of the four big guns firing an almost perfect broadside rolled the ship away from the departing shells and then back again; the gun barrels automatically allowing for the movement and remaining fixed on the target.

*   *   *

Lying, hopefully hidden, in the jungle a matter of no more than five hundred yards to the east of where they believed the terrorists to be, the soldiers heard the whine of the big shells passing overhead a moment before their impact shook the ground even this far away.

"Challenger, this is Spotter. About three hundred yards over, can you come down a bit?"

The people on the bridge heard the voice from the loud speaker. The Captain nodded to Yeoman Houser.

"Spotter this is Challenger. Roger, will do. Out."

"Guns," the Captain spoke into the telephone again. "Can you come down about a hundred yards? Seems you're firing into the next county."

"Very Good Sir."

Those on the bridge couldn't hear what he said to the Transmitting Centre two decks below from where the guns were actually controlled but the four guns adjusted their elevation simultaneously.

"All guns ready, Sir."

"Thank you Guns. Shoot when you're ready."

"Main armament only Shoot. Shoot. Shoot."

Whilst the main armament were the only weapons likely to be used for bombardment, the Bofors anti-aircraft guns crews were also closed up on their weapons for exercise. As their Captain was wont to repeat ad nauseam, practice makes perfect and perfection saves lives.

"Challenger, this is Spotter. Nice one, Sir. Just close enough to wake them up but far enough on the other side of the river to suggest that they might be well advised to remain where they are. Over"

"Challengr, roger, out."

"OK Guns, seems you've got it just about right now. We'll try five rounds from each gun. That should put the fear of Christ up the enemy, not to mention what it will probably do to the poor bloody infantry who are supposed to be on our side; and it won't do your guns crews any harm, can't have them getting rusty.

"Yeoman. Advise Spotter that we will fire twenty rounds in five salvoes. He should be in communication with the ground also and can warn them to keep their heads down."

Naval gunnery is something slightly less than an exact science. Even in the best regulated of engagements, an occasional shell falls short, over or, on rare occasions, fails to explode when it does fall to earth. Today was no exception to this rule and just to make life interesting for all concerned, two 4.5 inch, high explosive shells fell a few yards short, landing in the river and causing something akin to a tidal wave.

"Challenger, this is Spotter. Two fell short, into the river. Quite a sight. Over."

"Yeoman. Tell spotter, 'sorry. Hope you didn't get your wings wet'."

*   *   *

Lying, hidden in the secondary jungle, what the Malays called the beluka, the soldiers waited, not knowing whether their next order would be to enter the real jungle, the tough, almost impassable rain forest, so dense a little further ahead that it blotted out the sun. Towards the camp, every thrusting creeper stretched upwards, searching for the sun that filtered through in faint streaks here and there, many of the trees were as straight as pillars, some hundreds of feet high. Alternatively, and hopefully, they would be ordered to remain hidden and allow the enemy to come to them. It all depended really on the amount of alarm and despondency caused by the navy. No alarm, they would have to move up and attack the presumably defended camp; lots of alarm and the enemy would do a runner. It was a matter of chance, for Sergeant Smith's inherited virgins, whether the runners came towards them or towards the other platoons spread in a semi-circle round the camp. The lieutenant took Owens' advice and offered up a short, succinct prayer; always worth a try, the sergeant had said.

It was the two short-falls that made up the minds of the terrorists who, until then, had been cowering under their huts in the hope that the flimsy structures would deflect anything other than a direct hit.

So far, the shells had been falling on the other side of the river and they hoped that the army thought that that was where the camp was located and would continue shelling the wrong place. Much of the water, blown out of the river by the two short-falls fell on to the camp and that made up the minds of the camp's inhabitants. The terrorists, recognising what they assumed to be a creeping barrage coming towards them, made a run for it away from the incoming shells. The army couldn't be everywhere and with luck enough of them would get through the army's cordon to regroup later.

It was a pity that their extra guns and ammunition hadn't arrived when expected. Had they done so, and with the additional men called in from other camps, they would not have been still here in the camp; they would have swept down upon the local villages and plantations and even the nearby tin workings in the rivers that fed the lake.

In doing so, they would have created havoc and demonstrated that defiance was futile, that the communists would always win; that the British would have to pack up and go as they had when the Japanese had come. As it was, there was no alternative but to run for it and reassemble at the alternative rendezvous in three days' time as per standing instructions.

Even the most experienced terrorist, when running for his life, cannot move silently and Sergeant Smith heard them coming towards his platoon. He could not risk making any noise to warn his men and could only hope that they too had heard what he had.

Five, black pyjama-clad, young Chinese broke through the jungle undergrowth in front of them, looking for the path that would allow them to escape. These were followed by a further four to their right. The lieutenant remembered, afterwards, thanking God that there were only nine of them and opened fire with his Sten gun; thirty-two rounds a minute and deadly at the range provided by the rapidly advancing Chinese. Moments later, the entire platoon opened fire, cutting the terrorists into small pieces. Stupendous waste of ammunition but they were only inexperienced kids, not proper soldiers yet. After this engagement perhaps?

"Cease firing."

His order, shouted at full bellow in order to be heard over the noise of the still shooting, terrified soldiers was heard by those nearest to him. As they ceased firing so too did those beside them until all was quiet.

Elsewhere, unseen, the shooting continued for some minutes before quiet returned. Not just quiet. Silence. Not a bird spoke, not a snake moved. All life sounds ceased for the few minutes it took for normality to return amongst all nature's things except the soldiers.

"Report, Sergeant."

Smith checked that the platoon was all present and correct.

"All present and correct, Sir."

"Thank God for that. It was a slaughter. They didn't stand a chance."

"No Sir, but neither would we if they had seen us first. This isn't the playing field of some minor public school, Sir. This is life or death and, if its all the same to you Sir, I'd rather it was their death, not mine."

"I'll vote for that Sergeant."

*   *   *

"Challenger, this is Spotter. Army reports that the camp has been abandoned and they have killed most if not all of the terrorists. Seems there were fewer than expected but I don't know how many that was so the information is probably useless. Army says thanks for your help. They'll buy the beer next time you visit. Over."

"Yeoman. Advise Spotter that we're always happy to oblige the army and mine's a double scotch."

"This is Spotter. Roger that. I'll pass it on."

"Secure main armament Guns. Stand down all guns crews. OK Pilot, where do we go from here?"

"On to Singapore Sir?"

"Could do, I suppose but I'd rather like to have another go at that junk."

"Will he be back, do you think Sir? We've destroyed the camp that was supposed to accept his delivery."

"But he doesn't know that Pilot. It might be worth our while stooging around a little. See what happens, as you might say."

"Then, I suggest that we move out to seaward to allow him room to make another attempt at the island."

"Good. You do that Pilot. Yeoman, see if you can still raise Spotter, will you, I'd like to talk to him.. Hallo Number One, come up to join the party?"

The First Lieutenant had come up from his action station in the Damage Control Centre where, happily, he had had nothing to do.

"Just wondered what luck we had, Sir. Did we actually hit anything?"

"Certainly Number One. Three trees."

"Oh I am glad, Sir. I'd hate to think all our efforts had been wasted."

"Captain Sir, I've got Spotter on here."

The Yeoman handed him the microphone.

"Hallo Spotter, this is Commander Powers. I wonder if you would do me a small favour? I seem to have lost a quite large junk during the night and I wondered if, fuel permitting, you could just take a quick jaunt up and down the coast a ways to see if he's hanging about just out of sight."

"Roger Wilco "

The tiny, high winged monoplane flew over the ship, dipping its wings in salute as it passed overhead.

"Do you really think he'll see anything, Sir?"

"Why not, Pilot. He's supposed to be a spotter, ain't he?"

"Very droll, Sir. But it might work. What if he finds two or three junks?"

"Then, Pilot, we go and look at all of them. The one we're looking for can do twenty-four knots so it is going to lie lower in the water than the normal junk without the weight of the engines. If our man has a full load of arms and ammunition on board too, he should be quite easy to identify. Anyway, Taff could do with some practice as Boarding Officer so he can go and take a look at all of them."

"He'll enjoy that Sir!" The First Lieutenant laughed.

"Like the rest of us Number One, he'll do as he's told. I don't want to have to explain to the Admiral that not only did I lose the damned thing the other night but that I made no subsequent effort to find the bugger."

"Challenger, this is Spotter. There's only one junk of any size in your area and that appears to be anchored just south of Kota Bharu. Can't see any activity either aboard her or near her but she's very close in where there's no apparent reason for her being there. Over."

The captain took the microphone from the yeoman. "Thank you Spotter, that's great news. Have a good flight home. I owe you one."

"Kota Bahru's about sixty five miles north of here, Sir."

"Well, don't just stand there Pilot. You're the officer of the watch, take me there."

"Aye aye, Sir."

*   *   *

The jungle made progress difficult but helped Cho to avoid discovery. He had remained in the camp, underneath one of the huts when the others bolted. Although they had followed their instructions to divide into small groups of no more than five and to leave the camp gong in all directions, he had heard the shooting to the east of the camp and drawn the conclusion that

156

that was where the majority of the army was waiting for them.

The water in the fast-moving river was cold, in spite of the ambient temperature. The spring that fed this small river was not more than a mile or so upstream and the water issuing from the ground was much colder than the surrounding air.

Cho waded as far across the river as he could, then struck out for the far bank. Westwards, he hoped he would be able to avoid any soldiers who had by-passed the camp to get to the other side of the river. Perhaps they had crossed higher up or even approached from the road far to the west but that would have been a very long haul without any guarantee that it would have been worthwhile.

No, on reflection, he was convinced that the army would have arranged for the high-explosive shells to be fired over the top of the camp to drive the men therein either towards the waiting army or persuade them to remain where they to put up some defence; a defence that would inevitably have been unsuccessful.

He lay silently at the edge of the jungle on the western side of the river, waiting, listening for any sign of the army. Others had run to the west also but had not stopped to assess the situation but had fled deep into the jungle in which they hoped to hide themselves until the army got tired of searching and went home to their barracks. Even this close to the riverbank, he had seen the bodies of two of his men who had been killed by the high explosive shells. He cursed the British in both Chinese and English.

He would wait; all day if necessary. When the way was clear, he would make his way by a circuitous route not back to the camp but to his mother's house in Terengganu. He would be safe there until he could organise the regrouping of the men who would dribble back to the camp when they felt that it was safe to do so. It would not be for some days yet; he had time to get himself cleaned up.

FIFTEEN

Cho didn't look his usual smart self when, late at night, he opened the door of his mother's house. His black pyjama-style suit was torn and dirty and his feet were badly cut and bruised. He stood, looking over the old woman lying on her bed.

"You didn't warn us."

"Of what, son?"

"That the soldiers were coming yesterday morning."

"I did not know."

"Why did your daughter in law not tell you?"

"It is possible she didn't know my son."

"But she is the woman of the English Sergeant. He would have told her if he was going on patrol. He always has."

"Then you must ask your wife but first, let me get you food and water. You must wash and change if you are to walk safely about the town."

He sat. His head lolling back against the wall. His mother saw his feet and went to fetch water with which to wash them. Perhaps, she thought, when the blood was washed away they would not be as badly cut as they at first appeared. But by the time she returned he was asleep. She left him. Tomorrow he would feel refreshed and he could bathe and change into his town clothes before going to see his wife.

*   *   *

From seaward, the radar showed nothing but the general background clutter that he expected. Petty Officer Flowers shortened the range a little and some of the clutter fell away, leaving echoes only from the larger objects on shore and a single small contact that appeared to be just a few yards offshore. Could be a rock, of course, he told the bridge.

"Yes, I suppose it could but the chart shows nothing immediately off shore here so it could be our junk."

"Right Number One. Call away the boat's crew and boarding party. Taff," he turned to Lieutenant Evans beside him, "don't take any chances. I want him searched and if he's the one I hope he is, I want him arrested. We'll be almost alongside so don't take any nonsense from him."

"Very good, Sir."

"OK Pilot, take us closer in but try not to run us aground on anything. Guns, I want a warning shot just beside him. Close enough for him to know that if we wanted to hit him we could. I don't want him trying to do a runner, I don't want him sunk, I want him arrested and taken back to Singapore."

"Aye aye Sir. Scare him but don't hurt him. I understand."

The explosion, just to starboard and ahead of the anchored junk made it plain that the warship meant him to stay where he was. Lieutenant Wo considered for just a moment the possibility of flight and even of resistance but there was no way out for him. Whichever way he tried to run they could shoot holes in him and, although he was pretty sure that they didn't want to sink him, he suspected that, once close enough, they could put a few shells through the engine compartment. That, as they say, would be that. Funny, he thought. Quite often, when in trouble or dealing with a problem, he thought in English expressions.

There was just one possible way in which he might frustrate their intentions. In a wooden vessel such as his, even a small fire would quickly develop into a conflagration; the masts, rigging and rattan sails would burn first of course but, if the navy so much as suspected that he was carrying ammunition, they would not dare to come close. With luck, the junk would sink before the fire actually reached the cargo and, in this shallow water, this could be recovered later.

The warship had stopped about half a mile away and lowered a boat that was already coming towards him. In it, he could see, armed men ready to board his vessel. Unable to avoid the capture of his ship, he determined to prevent its cargo being lost to the cause. He gave a friendly wave towards the incoming boat and while waiting for them to arrive instructed his tiny crew.

"Quickly, bring all your bedding aft and place it in the cabin. Also, anything else that will burn easily." He turned towards the on comingboat.

"Welcome aboard Captain," he said.

"Lieutenant Evans, Royal Navy," the lieutenant said. "I intend to search your ship for contraband. Do you intend to resist?"

Wo glanced at the fifteen armed men standing on the deck behind their officer. "That would be foolhardy in the extreme." he said. "Please carry on. You won't mind if I don't accompany you? I already know what cargo I am carrying. I shall remain in my cabin."

Evans was impressed by the English being spoken by the junk's captain. He'd never before met a junk captain who spoke English both properly and with such facility.

"May I ask where you learned English, Captain."

"Hong Kong. I was born there and grew up there. Now, if you would get your search done, I will be able to proceed to Kota Bharu and unload my timber."

The boarding party had split up and were looking into every nook and cranny. There was only a small storage locker under the bow and the large hold amidships. Astern of that, the large cabin offered the only other place that anything could be hidden.

Wo turned and opened the door but Taff Evans preceded him. In the semi darkness of the cabin's interior, there appeared to be nothing untoward. A bunk, what appeared to be an English style toilet bowl and little else. A brazier and a large sack of charcoal stood in one corner which seemed unusual in that cooking would normally have been done out on the deck, away from anything that might catch fire but, perhaps it was kept here to protect it from the rain that would come later this afternoon. Also, unusually, there appeared to be various other items, rush mats and the like, that would, Taff believed have normally been kept in the for'ard locker and used by the crew for sleeping on deck.

The trap door in the cabin floor, leading down to the diesel engines' compartment, was hidden by a rush mat that covered almost the entire area but Evans had been briefed to look for it. If she was the junk equipped with diesels, there was only one place they could be and that was beneath the after cabin where

162

a small part of the hold had been partitioned off to accommodate them.

The rush matting was rolled up and pushed forward, against the wooden bulkhead, knocking over the sack of charcoal. Two members of the boarding party, the stokers sent especially for this purpose, went below to examine the engines and to disable them to prevent any attempt at escape. Watching, Wo let them go below then lit a cigarette. Throwing the still burning match into the rush matting he strolled out on to the deck, closing the door behind him.

He caught the eye of the three crewmen standing on the deck, keeping out of the way of the searching sailors who were removing the battens holding down the tarpaulin covering over the hold. He directed his eyes first to the port bulwark and then to the beach some hundred and fifty yards away. They nodded and moved slowly towards the ship's side. Lieutenant Evans smelled burning at about the same instant that the for'ard bulkhead of the cabin burst into flames.

"Under below!" He shouted down through the trapdoor. "We're on fire, get yourselves up here."

He threw himself at the cabin door before realising that it opened inwards. The two stokers climbed out of the engineroom and, holding the single blanket from the bunk before them as a heat shield, grabbed the door handle and pulled it open.

On deck, one member of the boarding party stood looking down into the hold into which the other sailors had descended, having exposed enough of a hole to allow them entry.

"Get them out of there!" Evans shouted to the man, who glanced over his shoulder to see who was shouting. The sailor's eyes widened as he saw the flames now rising brightly and fiercely from the after end of the vessel. "Get the others up out of there!" Evans shouted again.

The sailors tumbled out of the hold and instantly recognised the danger they were in. "Find something to hold water and try and douse these flames. We must keep her afloat if we can. "Martin," he shouted to the signalman. "Signal the ship and tell them the junk is on fire and that we are trying to put out the flames. Rogers," he turned to the man who had been left on deck when the others had gone below, "where are the crew?"

Don' know, Sir. They was here a moment ago."

Evans looked over the side in time to see the four men swimming strongly for the shore. He considered the possibility of hitting them with gunfire from the burning junk and decided that saving the ship must come first.

Buckets were found and ropes attached so that they could be thrown over the side, filled with water and hauled back up again and the water thrown on to the burning bulkhead. "Quick," he ordered. "Quick as you can with the water. You, Rogers, come with me, we have to bring down the bulkhead before it sets fire to the deckhead, the chicken coop and the mast and sail above that. If that falls into the hold, we're in real trouble."

"What about the diesel fuel down below, Sir. Won't it set fire to that?"

"Not if we're lucky, Rogers. It's very difficult to set fire to diesel oil as long as it's cold and our fire is burning upwards, not down, so come on."

They attacked the blazing planking with whatever they could lay hands on. Rogers found a marlinspike and Evans what was obviously intended to be a fire axe. They attacked the bulkhead at its weakest point, between the planks that were actually burning; tearing the planks away and throwing them over the side as they came free.

By the time the fire was out and the last of the smouldering wood and bedding thrown over the side, the junk's crew had disappeared into the trees that lined the shore. Signalman Martin lifted his Aldis lamp, flashed a R to the ship and reported to Lieutenant Evans.

"Captain says to ignore the crew and put out the fire if you can, Sir."

"Why, thank you Martin. I had rather hoped that that would be his advice." The irony was lost on Martin.

"Please advise the ship that the fire is now out and that the crew have got ashore and buggered off into the trees. We will continue the search and report."

They removed the rest of the tarpaulin covering the hold cover and removed the hold cover itself so that they could more easily see what was down there. Timber; that was what was down there, lots of timber. Below the timber, case upon case of automatic rifles, ammunition, hand grenades and not a few limpet mines; enough to support a small war, which was precisely what it was supposed to do.

"Signalman, please advise the ship that we have found enough armaments to start world war three and request instructions."

The Aldis signal lamp clacked and clicked as the trigger moved the mirror within it up and down to direct and misdirect the light towards and away from the eye line of the signalman in Challenger.

"Reply Sir. Ensure fire is totally out and prepare to be taken in tow."

"Thank you. Right, Petty Officer Barber, see if you can find something up for'ard to which we can attach a tow. If all else fails, I suppose we can always use the foremast and lead the tow out through the anchor hawse. She'll tow like a bloody porpoise but it will have to do if we can't come up with anything better."

Ashore, Wo, watching, saw that his plan had failed. He had hoped to burn the junk down to the waterline and make the boarding party abandon her. With luck, she would have sunk, settled slowly and gently on to the sandy bottom with her cargo intact and recoverable without difficulty. Instead, he watched his junk slowly move away from the shore, snagging a bit but finally falling in astern of the destroyer as the slack was taken up in the tow.

He turned to his crew, angrily. "Get lost. Go in different directions and don't come into Kota Bharu until tomorrow. Make contact through the company's agent on the dockside, you know where he is?"

They nodded.

"Good."

In Challenger, Lieutenant Evans reported to the bridge, having been relieved as commanding the towing party aboard the junk by Lieutenant Brothers, an enthusiastic yachtsman and perfectly capable of sailing the junk should the tow fail for any reason.

"Well, Taff, that was very well done."

"Thank you Sir. It was a bit hairy for a while until we got the fire under control and we lost the crew too. A bit tricky when it's not your ship and you don't know where anything is. I'm afraid young Rogers has rather badly burned hands, he was tearing at the planking without any protection but I gather that the sick bay tiffy can sort him out. At least he'll be excused watches for a few days, eh? Can't be all bad."

"I can only hope that he agrees with you Taff. I'll see him later and thank him for his efforts. What about the rest of the boarding party? Any other casualties?"

"No Sir. A few bruises and scratches and, oh yes, Petty Officer Barber says he's strained his shoulder and thinks he should lie down for a week or two."

"That sounds about par for the course. I'll see all of them in my cabin in an hour, OK?"

"Very good Sir."

*   *   *

Lieutenant Wo, of the People's Republic of China Naval Force, found the path he was looking for, running more or less parallel with the coast, and walked towards the small town of Kota Bharu and the shipping company's agent, Ah Lee. He would have to report failure but there was nothing he could have done that he had not done. He had escaped from the warship waiting off the island rendezvous and had thought himself free and clear but somehow, the British warship had found him. There had been no possibility of escape and his attempt to sink the ship and its cargo in a position from which it could be reclaimed had been unsuccessful but he could have done no more.

It was a long walk but he was in no hurry. Tomorrow morning would be the best time to go and see the agent at Kota Bharu, when the port was open and there would be others on the dockside. He would walk for an hour or so and then find somewhere to lie down and get some sleep.

SIXTEEN

The junk slewed to starboard at the slightest provocation, causing the tow to snatch taut and sag alternately due to it being taken out through the port hawse hole. She had no bullring in the bow and there was no provision for being towed in her design.

There was no way of preventing this behaviour other than constant attention to the steering. Keep the junk as docile as possible and keep the tow taut; any slack and she would yaw and snatch.

"Signal from the tow, Sir." Leading Signalman Hawkins handed the clipboard to the officer of the watch, Lieutenant Evans.

Evans read it and opened the weather lid on the voicepipe to the captain's cabin.

"Captain, Sir, signal from the junk. Almost impossible to maintain present towing speed without danger; suggests that they let go the tow and we let him use either the diesels or the sails to move the ship."

"Thank you Taff, I'll think about it."

He was reluctant to let go of the junk as, in the event of foul weather, always a possibility they could lose contact and even lose the junk itself. With its inexperienced prize crew, he preferred to hold on if he could. On the other hand, relieved of the tow, Challenger would be more able to keep station on her, be free to manoeuvre as necessary and to take any necessary action required.

He pressed the bell button on the wall in front of him summoning his steward. "Ask the first lieutenant to come and see me, will you Masters."

"Sir?" The first lieutenant stood in the doorway.

"Come in Number One. As you know, the damned tow is giving us a lot of trouble and young Brothers suggests that he should either sail her back to Singapore or use her diesels. Don't know if she has enough fuel to motor all that way and whilst that would certainly save both of us a lot of trouble, I'm loth to let her go and risk our being separated. What do you think?"

"I think it's a very good idea Sir but he will need a larger crew if he's going to sail her."

"But you can arrange something without too much difficulty."

"Yes, Sir. The junk is normally crewed by three or four men but allowing for our sailors not being experienced junk sailors exactly we shall need a crew of at least nine. That will allow for a proper west-country-three watch schedule to be established and allow the off-watch men to sleep. I'll sort something out."

"Thank you. I'll tell Brothers that he can expect additional crew this afternoon. And Harry, see if you can find some sailors who actually know something about sailing in sailing boats, eh?"

"I'll do my best Sir."

"And don't forget the extra food and a chef, eh?"

The first lieutenant returned to his tiny office and sent for the Buffer, the chief bosun's mate.

"Buffer, "he said when that man arrived. "I need to send a sailing crew over to the junk. You know, sailors who know something about sails and the like."

"Not a lot of 'em about Sir but I'll see what I can find out. How long have I got?"

"Say an hour? Then I'll try and work out who can be spared and who can't."

The traditional Chinese junk is rigged in much the same way as an old-fashioned thirty-two-foot naval cutter with a lugsail on each mast. There should, the chief bosun's mate thought, be enough men onboard who had crewed such a boat, even if only when in basic training. Some of the big ships still carried them and they were used in regattas in peacetime and as lifeboats should the need arise. The quickest way to find out was probably to go round to each mess and ask.

Lieutenant Brothers recognised what it was that was worrying him; not professionally but personally. He hadn't been to the lavatory properly since boarding the junk and he wanted to go now.

Satisfied, he tore off some sheets of paper, surprised that the Chinese captain had both a European lavatory and paper, and leant forward; the whole edifice leant forward with him. He leant back again and the whole thing returned to the horizontal. He stood, performing the operation needed and threw the paper into the bowl. He pressed the lever down and the lavatory flushed, carrying everything away into the sea through the side of the ship.

The cistern was mounted on the bulkhead behind the bowl and fed by a hand pump with seawater through a flexible hose. Gently, he pulled the cistern towards him. The whole section of bulkhead came away, tipping the bowl forward and exposing the cavity below. "Well I never," he said to himself. "Now that's cute."

He examined the radio in the secret compartment, calling for the signalman. "OK Bunts, what do you think of this then?"

"Well Sir, in the seven years I've been in the Andrew, I've heard a lot of shit come out of the radio but I've never actually been able to shit into one myself."

"Very funny. What I mean is, do you know how to work this thing?"

"Afraid not, Sir. You need a sparker."

"Yes, we do, don't we. Interesting eh? I wonder who he was in radio contact with?"

"Well, sparks will be able to see what frequency it's set at and we might be able to simply switch it on and listen; see what develops."

"We'd better tell Challenger what we've found and ask them to let us have a sparker in the additional crew they're sending."

He was glad that Challenger had agreed to cast loose the tow and allow them to sail the junk home to Singapore. It would be a novel experience, not only for him but for the Royal Navy also. He wondered how many other officers would be able to lay claim to having commanded a Chinese junk under sail, having first captured it from the enemy? Well, perhaps he hadn't personally captured it but Challenger had and he was the prize captain. It would do him no harm when his half-ring was due; not to mention the possibilities for telling his tale to wardroom audiences willing to buy his gin.

"Petty Officer Barber. Prepare to let go the tow. We are going to sail her in."

"What, up the Johor Strait and into the naval base, Sir?"

Barber could just visualise the assembled sailors gathered to witness this evolution, all laughing and pointing at them as they struggled to control this damn boat in the cross winds and the tidal currents at the entrance to the dockyard.

"Yes, Barber. Right into the dockyard and in a sailor-like manner too!"

"Well, we'll do our best, I'm sure, Sir."

*   *   *

Refreshed by some hours' sleep and bathed, Cho dressed and ate the food his mother provided. "What are you going to do?" she asked.

"I'm going to see my wife and I'm going to find out why she didn't warn us of the attack. I don't know how many of my men survived, not many I suspect and we must certainly postpone the attacks we had planned. I am not happy, mother, not at all happy."

"You will not hurt her?"

"Not more than necessary to obtain the information that I need, Mother. You need have no fear for her, she will still have a use in the future."

He didn't want to go to his wife's room until later in the day and he spent the rest of the morning walking round the town, hoping to see men from his group blending into the background amongst the many Chinese traders and labourers busily going about their usual business.

He saw none. Whether this was because there were none or because those that had managed to reach the town had successfully blended into the constantly moving mass of people that the town supported he didn't know, but with every passing hour he became more angry with his wife.

She had failed him, she had failed the cause and, very probably, she had warned the English sergeant that the Malayan Communist Party's freedom fighters would be ready for them when they attacked, as they would have to now that the position of the camp was known. The local police spies found it by interrogating one of the villagers who brought them food.

*   *   *

It was late, almost sunset before the enlarged prize crew was organised and transferred to the junk. "OK sparks, what can you tell me about this little gem?" Lieutenant Brothers showed Leading Telegraphist Morgan the lavatory radio.

Morgan sucked through his teeth. "Not a lot, I'm afraid Sir. Simple enough piece of kit, this here is the on/off switch, appears to be battery powered so the transmitting range won't be all that far. Let's see what sort of an aerial it's got, then we can assess its receiving range more accurately."

Out on deck, he looked upwards at the masthead, looking for some sort of aerial. Yes. There it was, better than he had expected really. A long aerial, stretched between the two mastheads. At that height and that length, even with only what he assumed to be twelve volts of power, he reckoned the radio could have a transmitting range of perhaps fifty or more miles and a receiving range of some hundreds of miles, depending upon the power of the transmitter.

He returned to the cabin and examined the dial settings. "Ah, Sir. Its set at a fixed frequency, probably receive only but I reckon a powerful transmitter some hundreds of miles away could be received. Not enough power to transmit over much more than, say, fifty miles though."

"So, you say it's set for receive only?"

"It seems so, Sir. Of course, I could change that, all you have to do is move this switch. The instructions are in Chinese but the set is pretty standard kit and I'd have no trouble operating it if you want, Sir."

"No. I think we should leave it on receive but, as we don't know when or how often he receives his instructions, we could run down our batteries without hearing anything. Better tell Challenger what frequency this thing is set on and let them listen."

"Right Sir. Does that mean you don't need me onboard?"

"Why? Don't you like yachting?"

"On the whole, Sir, I'd rather sleep in my own hammock in my own mess."

"Well, hard luck Morgan, you stay. I'm sure that Petty Officer Barber will be able to find a job for you."

*   *   *

Cho climbed the stairs to Molly's room and opened the door without knocking. The room was empty. Of course, he told himself, she'll be at the bar. He left, closing the door behind him and turned down the side street towards the bar; Sally Hun, a friend of Molly's, saw him go.

The hissing sound of Tilley lamps now came from many of the shops that lined the street and from the bar itself although the inside room, the room used by the owner as accommodation, had a single electric bulb suspended from the ceiling and a circulating fan designed to move the humid air, though it was so inefficient that it served only as a status symbol for the owner; a symbol of his obvious affluence and importance.

Molly saw him and indicated that he should sit at the table furthest from the hissing lights. What shadow there was would help to hide his face, even if it was obvious that he was there. People would notice that a Chinese was sitting in the bar; that was unusual in a bar usually used by British soldiers. Happily, there were none there at the moment; it was early yet.

"We must talk."

"I can't leave now, the owner will want to know why."

"Is your Sergeant coming to see you today?"

"No, he is in camp, waiting to go on the big patrol that I told you about."

."Idiot! The big patrol was two days ago. They attacked our camp with heavy artillery and even an aeroplane. It was a slaughter, I was lucky to escape with my life. Why did you not know? You should have known."

Her heart leapt, was it possible that her sergeant was alive, that he had not been killed? Deep within her, she knew that it was important that he was alive and that she would see him again. She returned Cho's glare, matching his venom with her own. She was glad that she had lied to her mother in law, she had been right to do so, she knew now that she loved her sergeant and owed nothing to Cho. She stood straight, looking him in the eye.

"I haven't seen him for days. Perhaps it was all changed and he didn't know."

"I am not a fool. Of course he would have known and he would have told you. Why did you not tell me?"

"I didn't know, Cho. Really."

"I do not believe you. You will come with me now. You can explain to your employer when you get back that you had to visit family urgently."

"Where are you taking me?"

"You will come to my mother's house and you will explain why you did not warn us of the attack."

He was obviously very angry; she had never seen him like this before. But told that she was being taken to her mother in law's house, Molly relaxed and followed him into the darkness outside the glare of the hissing lamps. Her mother in law knew that the sergeant had not been to the bar for some days and that she had already passed on all the information she had to her for Cho. She was glad she had not told her mother in law about the change of date, perhaps her Sergeant was still alive; she hoped so.

He stopped, pushing her into the alley behind a row of closed shops. She saw the knife only a second before it pierced her heart. She dropped the tiny bag she carried, the bag in which she kept those things necessary for a girl and the few dollars she had earned in tips so far that day.

Cho kicked her angrily, relieving a little of his anger, and pushed her body behind a pile of empty boxes which smelled of rotting vegetables.

"Bitch." He said. "Traitorous bitch. You liked your English Sergeant too much."

The whole thing had been silent; nobody saw or heard anything. He walked away. Bitch! She had failed to warn him, she had allowed the British soldiers to kill most, possibly all of his men, he didn't know. Tonight, he would kill any soldier that he met, he would take a life for a life even if he didn't know how many that must be. He would kill every soldier drunk enough or careless enough to wander about the town on his own. In the morning, he would feel better.

*   *   *

In the wireless office in Challenger, P.O. Tel. Charlie 'Gene' Autry half listened to the atmospherics on the speaker above his desk. Tuned to the Chinese frequency, he would hear anything transmitted. Beside him sat the youngest and most fluent in English of the laundrymen carried by the ship for the convenience of both officers and men.

They had their own tiny mess down aft where they had installed a huge wash tub and a drying cupboard; it wouldn't do for one of His Majesty's war ships to be seen sailing along with washing hanging from the guardrails or from improvised washing lines but cleanliness is next to Godliness and the dhobying had to be done by someone. On the whole, the sailors preferred that it was done by the Chinese laundrymen rather than doing it themselves.

Taken onboard at Hong Kong, these men were not on the ship's books but were there officially as supernumeraries. Chin, the young lad sitting beside Autry, hoped one day to be able to join the Hong Kong water police and was keen to practice his English.

"OK Chin, You know what you have to do? If anyone speaks Chinese on that speaker up there, you write it down on that pad, OK? You can translate it later."

"Yes PO, I understand. But what if it's not in my dialect? I speak Cantonese, if the man on radio is from another province, I may not understand him."

"Then, Sunny Chin, we are all in trouble. We'll just have to hope that he uses Mandarin, that's the official Chinese language, ain't it?"

"Yes PO, Mandarin I understand also."

"Good." He offered the boy a cigarette.

Astern but within range of the ship's radar, the junk sailed with no lights showing other than the one white light at the forward masthead. This told any other vessel that saw her that she was moving and that she was a small vessel; larger vessels would wear two lights, one on each masthead in accordance with international practice, plus port and starboard navigational lights.

"She seems to be sailing pretty well, Number One. Perhaps young Brothers has missed his vocation."

The first lieutenant smiled in the darkness on the bridge. "I doubt if he ever expected to be sailing a Chinese junk, Sir."

"No, Harry, I don't suppose he did but the experience won't do him any harm."

Sitting in his sea chair, the captain was at peace with the world, or that part of the world that immediately surrounded him. In a few minutes, he would go below to his cabin and write another page of his letter.

They would be in Singapore in two days, the junk was limited to about four or five knots under sail and Challenger had to stay in company just in case something went wrong. The lowest calculated speed for the ship was six knots at forty-six revolutions on each engine and to go slower than that was a matter of trial and error. At the moment the engineroom telegraph indicated thirty-nine revolutions and the log indicated a speed through the water of just over four and a half knots.

"If we get any weather during the night," he told the officer of the watch, Lieutenant Darling, "we'll need to keep a very keen eye on our friend back there. Don't want to lose him."

"I'll make a note in the log Sir and pass it on to my relief."

"Oh, and let me know at once if we hear anything on that radio frequency we're monitoring."

"Yes, of course, Sir.

"Right then. I'm off down for my dinner. Are you going down Number One or are you so enthralled, so captivated by the beauty of the evening that you are going to stay up here all night?"

"I'll be going down shortly Sir. There's a couple of things I want to check before dinner."

"Right ho."

He went down the ladder at the back of the bridge to his cabin two decks below.

"Right, Pilot. Who have you got on the radar? Obviously Petty Officer Flowers can't keep constant watch."

"No Sir. He's put Leading Seaman Booker on for the First watch, Able Seaman Jones will take the Middle and Flowers himself will take the morning just to make sure that she is still there."

"Right. Let me know if the junk signals, won't you."

"Of course Sir."

"Then I'll go down. I'll be in the wardroom if you need me."

"Very good Sir."

*   *   *

Lieutenant Brothers, in the junk, was eating a sparse supper. Not quite what he might have expected in the wardroom aboard Challenger but adequate. Corned beef, fried potatoes and baked beans. The catering facilities on the junk were somewhat limited by western European standards but the chef had done his best. His problem, so he said, was that the Chinky crew only ate rice and bits of fish all boiled up together in one pot and all helped themselves from that pot. Not quite what a British officer would expect.

Most of the rest of the prize crew were scattered about the upper deck, leaning on the bulwark staring at their ship in the distance and wishing they were aboard her in their proper mess and comfortable, but a few were sitting just for'ard of the hatch, playing cards. Not for money of course, that would be illegal and frowned upon by Petty Officer Barber who, equally certainly, never broke the rules himself.

"That's five Dollars you owe me, Charlie. You can pay me on payday."

"Yeah, right. That's if I don't win it back before we get to Singers."

"No chance son. You don't know how to play poker; you just thinks you do."

"OK Hooky, we'll double the stake on the next hand and see who knows how to play."

"You're an idiot Charlie but if you insist, who am I to refuse to take your money." He dealt the cards. "What do you bet on that hand, then?"

"Don't know yet, do I? I'll take two."

Standing in the darkness by the mainmast, Petty Officer Barber elected not to hear any of this discussion. It was none of his business if the fool and his money were soon parted. Well, technically, it was his business but if he didn't hear them betting, he couldn't be expected to break up a perfectly innocent, friendly game of cards, could he?

*   *   *

The loud speaker in the wireless office sprang into life. A flow of hurried Chinese could be heard all over the office as the PO Tel turned down the volume. Christ. The transmitter was either right beside them or it was a very powerful transmitter indeed. Young Chin picked up the pencil and wrote as quickly as he could.

When he had finished, the PO Tel, called up the voicepipe to the bridge. "Bridge, Wireless office. We've received and copied a broadcast on the frequency we're monitoring and Chin is trying to translate it into English. It may take some time, I'll let you have a copy when he's finished."

"OK Pots. I'll tell the officer of the watch."

Jim Sallis reported to Lieutenant Darling who, in turn, spoke down the voicepipe to the captain's cabin.

"Thank you Pilot. Let me see whatever it turns out to be. OK?"

"Very good Sir. Bridge Messenger."

The able seaman messenger of the watch moved from his loafing position at the back of the bridge. "Sir?"

"Tell the first lieutenant that we have received a signal on the Chinese frequency and that it's being translated. He's in the wardroom."

*   *   *

Cho was angry with himself, although now calmer than he had been earlier, He needn't have killed his wife. It was possible, he now admitted to himself, that she had not known about the change in dates for the attack. Anyway, they had not yet received the supply of arms and ammunition that his mother had told him should be here by now. He must ask her about that too. Was it possible that both his wife and his mother had deserted the cause? Was it possible that they believed it to be unachievable? He would challenge his mother when he got home, meanwhile, he would kill a soldier; it would make him feel better.

*   *   *

In Challenger, young Chin laboured over his translation of the signal he had received, taking great care to ensure that it was both accurately translated and clearly and neatly written in English. Perhaps this would help him when he applied to join the water police back in Hong Kong, perhaps they would consider this an additional and useful qualification. His father would be happy. A son in the water police would be a useful source of intelligence when he undertook the occasional smuggling operation for the triad to whom he owed so much money. He was a good sailor but as a gambler he seldom won against the house. Nobody did!

SEVENTEEN

The translation completed, Petty Officer Autry thanked young Chin and told him to continue listening, just in case there was another broadcast, specifically for the junk. What the Chinese had translated was what would, in the Royal Navy, be described as a meat and spuds signal; routine information and advice, obviously addressed to a lot of ships. That, in itself, was interesting but not particularly helpful. He took the transcription to the Captain's cabin and knocked on the doorpost.

"The Chinese signal, Sir. Nothing interesting but it does indicate that there is more than one of their ships listening and the weather forecast indicates that they are all over the South China Sea."

"Thank you, would you show it to the first lieutenant, tell him I have seen it and don't think there is anything we need to do. Clearly, the junk was not expected to acknowledge receipt. Tell him that I suggest that we tell the junk that it was a lot of nothing and that they needn't worry about it. I suspect that this is the time for a regular broadcast to all ships and that any specific ship's signal would be transmitted immediately afterwards. Keep the frequency on speaker in your office PO Tel but I doubt if you will hear any more from it"

"May I keep young Chin Sir, just in case. He can sleep in the wireless office and I can give him a shake if he's needed."

"What does he think of that idea?"

"I haven't run it past him yet, Sir but it would be a pity to miss something useful."

"Very well but, remember, he's a civilian. If he says he wants out, out he goes, OK."

"As you say, Sir."

*   *   *

At four in the morning, Lieutenant Brothers looked around him. From the poop of the junk, the horizon was somewhat closer than it would be from the bridge of the destroyer but she was there, about two miles on his port bow and she would know if there was anyone else in the area. Petty Officer Barber had also arranged to be called for the morning watch and wished him good morning.

"Not a lot to see, Sir."

"No there isn't but, I imagine Challenger is keeping a good look out for both of us."

"We're not in any danger, are we Sir?"

"No, I shouldn't think so. The owners of this fine vessel don't know that they have lost her so we need fear nothing from them for the moment and Challenger has advised CinC that we are bringing her into Singapore so we needn't fear attack from our side either."

"I was wondering whether it might be a good idea for us to carry a white ensign just in case a police launch decides to come and take a look at us. I suspect that they know the position of most of the legal traffic going up and down this coast."

"I doubt that Barber. They didn't know where this damned boat was before we captured her or they would have done so themselves."

"Perhaps they were waiting to see where she was going, Sir."

"Yes, I suppose you could be right. Anyway, we can ask Challenger for a white ensign if it will make you happy."

Out of what little wind there was, the chef was lighting the charcoal brazier on which breakfast would be cooked. First, however, he would make large pot of coffee for the watch on deck

*   *   *

As was his custom, Commander Powers came up to Challenger's bridge to watch the sun rise. "Morning Number One. Going to be another glorious day, eh?"

"Morning Sir." The first lieutenant saluted the captain. "As you say, another beautiful morning. Now, if we could have this climate in England, we could all have saved ourselves the bother of joining the navy."

"That's a very profound thought for so early in the morning Harry. Don't tell me you are pining for home."

"Not what you would call pining Sir but one does feel the occasional pang of remorse at having left a perfectly good home to put ourselves in the way of other people's troubles."

"Alas, Harry, as a member of the United Nations and a member, no less, of that body's Security Council, I fear that Korea's problems are our problems also. Of course, I suppose the UK could resign from both and save us all a very great deal of money, even reduce the income tax, but I can't see our politicians relinquishing the prestige of our present position even if they have to bankrupt the rest of us to pay for it."

"Well, at least, Sir, they're paying for our refit and that means that we shall be in Singers for some months. Have you thought of suggesting that your wife joins you out here Sir?"

"It rather depends upon whether we shall, at the end of the refit, be based in Singapore, Hong Kong or sent back up to Japan and doing those everlasting patrols off the Korean coast. I can't very well ask her to spend six weeks or so coming out to Singapore and then, after a month or two at most, swan off up north again and leave her there."

"And I thought you were newly married Sir!"

"You may be a romantic Harry but I don't think my bank manager is. Have you any idea what it costs to come out here as a civilian passenger?"

"Must admit I haven't a clue, Sir."

"Well I have Harry and I can't afford it. Don't think I hadn't played with the idea though. I even suggested it in my letter but crossed it out later as being impractical."

"What are our chances of being based in Singers, do you think Sir?"

"Why Harry? Have you something in mind?"

"My fiancé is quite embarrassingly rich. I thought they might come out together. We could get married here and I could ask you to be my best man."

"I didn't know that Harry. That she is loaded I mean; you've never let on."

"Wouldn't do, would it Sir? It would sound like boasting or something worse."

"You're probably right Number One. Wouldn't do at all. It could spoil the atmosphere in the wardroom."

"Of course Sir. If she were to come out to marry me she could invite your wife to accompany her as some sort of chaperone; look after her virtue until after the ceremony and all that."

"Brilliant Harry but it wouldn't do, I'm afraid. I couldn't possibly allow my first lieutenant's fiancé to pay for my wife to join me. How would that look upstairs? "

"No Sir. I suppose not."

"No Harry. We'll just have to wait until we know what the future holds."

Below, in the wireless office, the telegraphists had been keeping watch on the Chinese frequency and with Chin's willing help, they had identified four other ships by their call signs. Petty officer Autry had compiled a report for the captain that he would give him this morning.

It had not been possible to determine where these other Chinese ships were nor what type of ship they were but they all appeared to be waiting for something to happen. Chin was sure of that but could come up with no suggestion of what that might be. Whatever it was, he thought that it might be due to happen in the next few days. The other ships had been instructed to return to base on completion of unloading. Chin thought that they must be cargo ships. Perhaps they were waiting for dockside space to become available?"

There had been no signals for the Flying Tiger either under that name or under the call sign that the telegraphist sent over to the junk had seen pencilled on the wall beside the clandestine radio set.

"OK Chin. Thanks for your help, I'll remember that and so will the captain. If I need you again, I'll call you but it probably won't be until this evening at the broadcast time. OK?"

"OK PO. You send for me when you need me, OK."

*   *   *

Kota Bahru, being a slightly larger and more important port than Terengganu further south, was awake and busy landing and selling the fish brought in by the overnight fishermen. These fishermen, who sailed at sunset and used Tilley lamps to attract fish to the surface during the night, usually returned at about daybreak and sold their catch to the waiting dealers or to anybody prepared to get up that early

This morning, a Chinese man that they didn't recognise stood on the wharf apparently waiting for something or someone. He was clearly trying not to be too obvious, but to the regulars he stood out like a beacon light.

Police Sergeant Lee had spotted him almost as soon as he had arrived. A stranger, any stranger would have been obvious immediately but most would have made some attempt to speak to someone on the busy wharf. This Chinese had not. Indeed, he had done exactly the opposite. He had tried to make himself invisible.

The sergeant watched him without making it too obvious that he was doing so. As was his custom, he took a tiny bowl of tea from the woman who stood by the Customs House every morning at this time, selling her tea to anyone who wanted it.

"He is a stranger, Sergeant," she said, looking out to sea. Should the stranger see them talking, it would appear as if they searching for another fishing boat or discussing the morning's catch.

"Yes Mother. Now I wonder why he wants to seem invisible?"

"If he buys tea Sergeant, should I ask him who he waits for? Tell him that I may be able to help him find whoever he waits for"

"No, mother. Do not expose yourself to possible danger. I shall watch him and when he meets whoever he is waiting for I shall know."

"He looks at the window of Chan Woo, the shipping agent; perhaps he waits for him."

"Then he has a long wait. Chan Woo does not enter his office until eight thirty and it is now only half past six."

"What joy it must be to be rich like Chan Woo, eh Sergeant?"

"That may be so mother, but we shall never know for sure."

"The stranger. He is smartly dressed but his clothes have been in the water."

"Yes mother. I had noticed. And it didn't rain last night. Not since four yesterday afternoon. Now I wonder why a man who can afford clothes like those could not afford to have them dried and pressed before coming into the town. Yes, mother, he is an interesting man. A man I must keep my eye on and report to my Inspector as soon as that other rich man is awake."

The old woman laughed, showing her broken, blackened teeth. Once, perhaps, she had been young and pretty but that must have been many years ago. The sergeant passed her a coin. "For your grandchildren," he said.

"You are a good man Sergeant. That was not necessary."

He strolled away, towards the main road, looking closely at all the boats that were alongside the wharf. To any watcher, he would be obviously going about his duties but no one on the wharf could leave it without his knowing it and no one could get on to the wharf without him seeing them. He could wait. Nobody was going to do anything at the moment.

At the gates of the wharf the watchman sat, tiredly watching those who were working. Soon he could go home and he could sleep properly. The sergeant greeted him loudly; he knew that the watchman was deaf although his employers didn't.

"Good morning Sen. You are awake?"

The watchman grinned up at the policeman. They had known each other since the police sergeant had been a boy, playing on the wharf.

"Of course. I am always awake. Nothing happens here without I know about it."

"Then, clever old man, who is the stranger loitering down by the customs house?"

"I have seen him before but he is a stranger. From a ship, maybe. Waiting for the custom house to open to declare something."

"He seems to be interested in Chan Woo's office."

"Ah, then perhaps he is waiting for a shipment to arrive. Perhaps it is late and he is anxious."

"There is no ship expected today old man. Nor was there yesterday. If his shipment is overdue, it is very much overdue and he would have been here before this."

"You have a suspicious mind, young Lee. I always thought so. Perhaps that's why you became a policeman."

"Perhaps so. Perhaps so but it is very early for such a man to be waiting here. If he knows Chan Woo, then he knows that he doesn't come to his office until half past eight and, if he doesn't know Chan Woo, then why is he watching that man's office?"

"Ah, young Lee. That is your problem. I shall go home in one hour and you will still be worrying. I am indeed a fortunate man am I not?"

"Yes, old man, you are thrice blessed. You will soon be going home to your breakfast and your bed, you will be paid an immense sum for looking after the wharf throughout the dangers of the night and thirdly, your employer will not know that you spent most of the night asleep. I shall not tell him but I do expect in return that you tell me anything that you do see or hear about this stranger."

"Sergeant Lee, you are a wicked man to threaten an old man like me but I will do as you say. We honest fellows must work together, eh?"

EIGHTEEN

With the dawn the island's village chief gathered six of the village's youngest men and led them along the path towards the camp.

It was quiet. There were none of the sounds he had expected to hear, the talk of the thirty men who lived in the camp, the banter of early risers demanding their tea and food from the cook; he had never been in an army but he knew how it was with young men who always woke hungry.

The camp was a mess. The huts had been set on fire and even the greenest wood would burn if given sufficient encouragement. Here it was obvious that dried grasses had been gathered and piled around the supporting legs under the huts. The up-draught had ensured that the dry floors above had burned fiercely, consuming all that had been within.

About the camp, the bodies of the dead terrorists lay as they had fallen, clearly no attempt had been made to search them for valuable watches or anything potentially saleable on the mainland. The young men set about ensuring that nothing of any value was wasted.

One of the searchers called out. "This one is alive. What should I do."

"Leave him. Check all the others."

There were no other survivors. Most of them had been hit by at least three bullets but the boy that had survived had been hit by only one, high in the thigh; he would not die from that if he received treatment. At least he had had the sense to play dead until the sailors had gone.

"Take this one back to the village, tell my wife to look after him. The rest of you, we must bury the dead, it is only right; we will bury them here."

The two biggest huts, the ones that had been mined, had ceased to exist. Among the debris many rounds of unexploded ammunition lay on the morning-damp ground.

"We must collect this and hide it," he told them, "it must not be found."

"There is the old cave in which we take shelter from the typhoons, we could hide it in there. Nobody goes there."

"Good. Do that then come back to the village. We must have a meeting; decide what we must do. We must ensure that the communists do not think that we had anything to do with this or that we helped in any way. My wife will tend the injured one and, when he is better, we shall send him back to the mainland to tell his friends that we saved his life and that it was the sailors that killed all the others."

*   *   *

In Terengganu, Cho looked at the knife he had used to kill three British soldiers last night, the one he had also used to kill his wife. He threw it into the muddy bottom of the monsoon drain at the side of the road.

He did not know where he had spent the night, only that this morning his head hurt and he had many bruises and two very deep cuts where his victims had tried to resist his thrusts. He would go to his mother's house; there he would be safe and he could bathe and change into clean clothes.

He remembered killing his wife Sun Lee, the girl that the British soldiers knew as Molly. No more British soldiers would know her; not now. She had deceived him. She had lied to him. She had chosen to protect her British sergeant and she had paid the price. Of the others that he had killed, he remembered only that he had killed more than one before exhaustion had claimed him and he had found a shelter in which to hide and sleep. His clothes were dirty and he would be noticed if he didn't hurry. His mother would hide him if there was any attempt to find the man who had killed the British soldiers. He imagined that the police would be asking questions in the town. He knocked on the door.

"What have you done?" his mother asked, seeing the bruises, the cuts and the filthy clothes. "What have you done my son?"

The first explanation for his condition that came to her mind was that he had murdered his wife but she must have fought back very strongly to leave Cho in this state.

"I have killed Sun Lee. She chose to protect her British sergeant by not telling me that the date for the attack had been brought forward."

"But you didn't get all those injuries killing Sun Lee."

"No mother. I also killed some British soldiers. I don't know how many."

"Wash yourself. I will prepare food. You look terrible. You must rest."

She went on to the small balcony on which the cooking stove was placed and broke eggs into a bowl.

"I will go into the town and listen to the gossip. If the police are looking for the soldiers' killer, you must stay here out of sight for a few days; until they get tired of looking."

The old woman scrambled the eggs and added them to some rice she had cooked the night before when she had expected Cho but he hadn't come. Now she knew why. She glanced back at her son. Was this what he had come to? He had gone too far. He had murdered his wife, the only person other than herself that had been genuinely fond of him, had ever shown him any kindness. He had become a wild animal.

*   *   *

It was a bad morning. Inspector Maples was in a bad mood. He didn't like mornings when he was greeted with the news that three British soldiers had been murdered in the town and that, just for good measure, a young Chinese woman's body had been found in an alleyway.

"Any chance the soldiers were killed for attacking the woman?"

"Doubt it Sir. The woman was found hidden behind some boxes outside a shop, the soldiers were found in three different areas and none of them anywhere near the woman."

"OK, usual routine enquiries in all the areas. Find out who they are and in the case of the woman, where she lived. I assume the soldiers were from the local camp?"

"Yes Sir. They have been identified and the army have removed them for medical examination, though its pretty obvious what killed them. They had deep knife wounds to the chest. Not much chance of survival, I would have said."

"Right. How about the woman?"

"Nothing yet but she was well dressed in the European manner so she must be living somewhere and in that case, sooner or later someone will miss her. Oh, and by the way Sir, the colonel said he would be happy to see you at any time. I think he meant when you know who did it."

"Did he now! OK"

*   *   *

Sixty miles north of that conversation, in Kota Bahru, and in another police station the morning was starting equally badly. Inspector Fredericks had only just reached his desk when the duty sergeant approached him.

"Sergeant Lee wants a word, shall I send him in?"

"Why hasn't he gone home? He was on the early shift wasn't he?"

"Said it was important Sir. Said he'd wait to see you."

"OK Send him in."

Sergeant Lee put down the magazine he had been reading. Perhaps he should have been reading the Police Gazette but he was too old for that, no longer ambitious.

"Well, Sergeant, what is it?"

"Yes Sir, I thought you should know. A stranger, Chinese about thirty, well dressed but dishevelled turned up on the wharf this morning at about half past six. Tried to make himself inconspicuous but by doing so, attracted the attention of all the regulars. One or two drew my attention to him although, of course, I had already seen him."

"So?"

"He was interested in Chan Woo's office but if he knew Chan Woo, he would have known that he doesn't arrive at his office before half past eight. I kept an eye on him and spoke to some of the other wharfites. One of them thinks he has seen him before but thinks he's from one of the ships that use the wharf. There are no ships at the wharf at the moment Sir."

"That's a fair enough report Lee but what significance do you attach to it?"

"I have left Constable Ho there to keep an eye on things and to report back when this stranger leaves."

"Right Lee. You have done all that you could. Go home and forget it. No doubt Ho will file a report and you can check it when you come on duty again tonight."

"I told Ho to report directly to you Sir. I think this is important but I don't know why. I'm hoping Ho will find out."

"Right, off you go Lee. I'll listen to whatever Ho has to report."

"Thank you Sir."

*   *   *

Sally Hun, Molly's friend, was worried. Molly had gone to work as usual yesterday and the man Cho, whom she recognised from previous visits, had let himself in to her room and then, realising that she wasn't there, had gone off again. Molly should have come back last night but she hadn't; neither had her British soldier friend, and that was unusual enough to arouse Sally's interest. She walked over to Molly's door and knocked. There was no answer; she hadn't expected one. She tried the door. It opened so she entered.

All was in order. The room was tidy as she had known it would be, Molly was a good girl, a clean girl and anyway, she had been in the room before at Molly's invitation so she had known what it would be like. Nothing appeared to have been touched or disturbed. Clearly the Chinese man friend she had seen enter yesterday had not searched the room or disturbed it in any way. Presumably he had been simply looking for Molly and finding her not there, had gone to look for her, perhaps where she worked. Perhaps she would go to the bar herself later if Molly didn't turn up.

At the fish shop this morning, she had heard that some British soldiers had been murdered in the town last night and she was worried about that too. Was Molly's sergeant one of them? It was no good, she would have to make enquiries.

*   *   *

Much to Petty Officer Barber's satisfaction, the white ensign now flew from an improvised staff at the stern of the junk. That was the proper order of things; she was, however temporarily, under Royal Navy command.

The weather forecast, passed from Challenger, was that a typical South China Sea storm was heading in their direction and that it would probably hit them during the night. Pity. One more day and they would be into the Johor Strait and within reach of the naval base. Ah well. It might be fun to ride out a storm in a junk, it was something he had never done. He wasn't sure how the others would enjoy it but that was their problem; as the navy always said, if they couldn't take a joke, they shouldn't have joined.

He was not worried about the ship, the design of which hadn't changed significantly in almost a thousand years. If it was that good, who was he to question its ability to ride out anything the South China Sea could throw at it with the possible exception of a full typhoon; any sensible sailor would get the hell out of the way of one of those.

"What if we go over to the diesels, Sir? Perhaps we could get down to Singers before the storm strikes."

Lieutenant Brothers gave this some thought. "You could be right PO. See if you can find out how much fuel there is in the tank, will you. Meanwhile I'll suggest it to Challenger; see what they say."

"Hey, Stokes." Barber called to the senior of the two stokers included amongst the prize crew in case they needed to use the engines. "How much fuel is there in the tank?"

"Quite a lot but as we don't know the capacity of the tank it's a little difficult to say exactly. Why?"

"Just wondered whether we had enough to get us down to Singers before this storm hits us, that all."

Leading Stoker Barrows turned to his fellow stoker. "What do you reckon Bob? How much fuel have we got?"

"Don't know Hooky but what if we run on diesels for a while? If we take a level now and again in say a couple of hours, we could establish some sort of rate of depletion. If the tank level doesn't drop like a stone, we might have enough."

"OK mate, you take a sounding now. Mark the dipstick in inches and then we can read off the depletion as a percentage of the total. If we don't have enough to get us all the way, the nearer we are to Singers, the happier I will be."

"Doubt if Brothers cares whether you're happy Hooky but it's worth a try, eh?"

The sounding in the tank produced a dipstick half coated with oil. "'bout half a tankful, wouldn't you say Hooky?"

"Yep. OK. I'll tell the skipper and recommend that we run on the engines for a couple of hours just to check it out. He probably won't mind that anyway, it'll let him test her abilities under power."

Brothers agreed that that was a logical and reasonable suggestion and, anyway, he did want to know how she handled under power. The rather crude steering system comprised a pair of wire ropes, one from each side of a shortened tiller bar, connected through simple pulleys to a central take-up boss on the wheel. The principle was sound enough in that, as you turned the wheel to starboard, the wire rope would be wound in from the port side rope and paid out to starboard, thus pulling the rudder to port. Whilst this system worked admirably on small boats, he was not convinced that it would be easy to handle such a large boat in heavy weather; in a heavy sea, it would be very difficult to turn the wheel against the pressure of the sea against the rudder. He thought that there should have been some sort of relieving tackle fitted to lessen the load but there didn't appear to be anything like that.

"OK stokes, we'll try it. I'll have to tell Challenger what we're doing or she will worry about us suddenly charging about under power, but I see no reason for them to refuse us permission to test the diesels."

Leading Signalman Hawkins saw the aldis lamp flashing from the junk and gave them a K to carry on with sending their message.

*   *   *

Sally Hun asked the owner of the bar, a clearly worried look on her face.

"She go away last night with Chinese man. Not seen her since. She bad girl, she work here. Soldiers come she not here, soldiers go away again to other bar. You tell her, she bad girl."

It was not like Molly to just go off like that without telling her employer where she was going or, at least, that she had to go somewhere. Where else? Perhaps her mother in law's house. Sally knew Molly was married and that her mother in law lived on the edge of the town, over by where the mangroves grew down to the sea. That was a Chinese part of town and she didn't know the name of Molly's mother in law.

She saw the policeman standing in the middle of the road directing what little traffic there was. He looked ridiculous standing there on his box waving his arms about when there were only two or three lorries and a bullock cart in sight.

Molly was her friend, a real friend. She would go to the police station, ask if there had been an accident or something. She hoped not.

The duty Constable told her that the Duty Inspector was away, out at the moment and that he wouldn't be back until late in the afternoon. Didn't she know there had been four murders in the town last night? Did she think the Inspector had nothing better to do than answer questions from some working girl that had lost a friend.

"I heard about soldiers being murdered. I'm sorry to bother you when you're busy."

"Just a moment girl. Who is your friend that is missing? What race is she?"

"Chinese, she is my special friend."

The constable knew that the woman who had been murdered was a Chinese.

"You wait here. I will find the Duty Sergeant. Perhaps he can help you."

Sally sat. It was cool in the police station. The fans kept the humidity down. In here, the fans ensured that, at least, the hot air moved about a bit.

"You have lost a friend, you say? A Chinese friend?" Perhaps the girl should be listened to.

"Sun Lee. She work in bar."

"How old is your friend Sun Lee?"

"Twenty eight, maybe a little older, difficult to tell. I mean she tell me she is twenty eight but we women, we all lie about our age."

The sergeant smiled. "Come with me."

Sun Lee's body was in the mortuary awaiting identification.

Sally screamed and the sergeant caught her before she fell in a dead faint. He helped her to a chair and waited for her to recover herself.

"That is your friend Sun Lee?"

"Yes."

"Come. We'll leave her in peace. We can talk in the office." He took her arm and led her towards the office in which he had a desk. "Sit. Do you want a glass of water?"

She placed the half-empty glass on the desk.

"Now, we must get this all in order. Firstly, what is your name?"

*   *   *

The dip stick reading after two hours running on the diesels at half throttle (they knew that at full throttle she would do more than twenty knots but would drink fuel like water) showed that just about an inch of fuel had been used. As there remained at least eighteen inches of fuel in the tank, the leading stoker felt safe in reporting to the lieutenant that he had at about thirty five hours at half throttle remaining; providing there wasn't too much sludge in the bottom of the tank. Say twenty four hours as a safe estimate.

"Thank you. I'll tell Challenger. That should do it nicely, I would think."

"Will we miss the storm, Sir?"

"No but we will be better able to ride it out if we don't have to keep brailing up and letting go the sails. If necessary, we can just head up into the wind and wait for it to pass."

*   *   *

The Inspector was in a bad mood when he got back from the army camp. He disliked pompous army officers who thought that they owned the world. He listened to the sergeant's report.

"So, we know who she is or was. What have you done about it?"

"I thought I should wait for your instructions, Sir. We know that she left work with a Chinese man last night at about seven and as, according to the autopsy, she was killed at about that time, he must have killed her. But, Sir, the friend didn't know who the man was nor where he lives."

"But we do know where she lived, don't we! Get a search party over there right away. I want to know all about her by tea time."

*　　　*　　　*

In Kota Bahru, a report from the constable who had been keeping an eye on the stranger visiting Chan Woo on the wharf lay on Inspector Frederick's desk.

The stranger had, it was reported, followed Chan Woo into his office and had been inside for more than an hour before leaving and going to the hotel at the end of the wharf where he had taken a room for three nights.

To call that place an hotel was, the Inspector thought, gilding the lily but to a constable he supposed anywhere that wasn't either a flop house for narcos or a brothel must be an hotel. No matter. He would walk past later and enquire about strangers who haven't arrived by ship; unusual to say the least.

After what the local army commander had told him earlier this morning, about the attack on a terrorist camp in the jungle only about sixty miles away down near Terengganu, any stranger was worth looking at. Well dressed but dishevelled was what sergeant Lee had said. Well, if he had come out of the jungle, he would be, wouldn't he?

Sergeant Lee had suggested that the man looked as if his clothes had been wet and allowed to dry on his back. Perhaps there had been a ship wrecked and he had swum ashore? That would have explained it. He would talk to Lee again tonight, before he visited the hotel. He had had a busy morning and was missing his afternoon nap; he was not the young man he used to be. He closed his eyes for a moment, an extended moment. It was a bad day and he suspected that it was going to get worse.

Lieutenant Wo didn't like the hotel, the room nor the risk of staying in town. He would much rather that Chan Woo had invited him to stay at his home to the north of the town. Worse, when the rest of his crew had turned up at Chan Woo's office he had sent them to the same hotel. Had the man no sense at all?

The sudden appearance of four unaccounted-for Chinese in the town would be noticed. Somebody would tell the police where they were. He would report Chan Woo's stupidity when he got back home.

He had instructed the three crew members to pretend that they didn't know him but he doubted if that would convince anybody, they would almost certainly be arrested for something and be questioned. He left the hotel and went in search of a drink. If he had to stay in town, then he might as well go to one of the bars where he might overhear the soldiers talking. He might learn something. What was more important was that he should not be arrested and that would be his primary consideration. He had reported to Chan Woo who would report back to China. He could now disappear until he could arrange his passage back to China. He had money.

*   *   *

Inspector Frederick's closed eyes didn't see the constable come into his office and remove the now cold but still full teacup.

NINTEEN

The sun was still both bright and hot, the steel of the ship's bridge was too hot to touch with comfort. In his corner, Leading Signalman Hawkins had one eye on the junk to starboard and the other on the officer of the watch, Sub Lieutenant Horton, the gunnery officer.

Guns had one eye on the captain sitting in his chair and the other on the giro repeater under the forebridge canopy. There was really very little for him to do, the helmsman in the wheelhouse would ensure that the ship maintained her course, the signalman of the watch, Hawkins, would ensure that if the junk signalled both he and the captain would know immediately and, on the port side of the forebridge, the navigator was working out the best course for the night. He relaxed.

"Satisfied, Guns?" The captain had been aware of his junior officer's tension and was reminded of his own days as a subby, waiting for his second ring to come through; desperate to appear competent and at the same time, determined to appear relaxed.

"Yes, Sir."

"Good. Wouldn't want you to have anything on your mind on such a beautiful day."

"Yes Sir."

When discussing gunnery, he was perfectly happy. He knew his stuff and was on top of his department. They were good and he was satisfied that there could be no criticism of them. As a watch-keeping officer, he was less sure. Competent? Yes but not quite as confident as he would have liked, that would only come with time. Still, as long as the Old Man was happy, he could reasonably expect his promotion to follow as the night followed day.

"What do you reckon Pilot. Will the storm hit us?"

"I'm afraid so Sir. At this speed there's nothing we can do to avoid it. I wouldn't like to be in the junk tonight though; going to get a bit rough I should think."

"Anything they can do about it?"

"The only possibility would be for them to run in amongst the islands at Mersing and hope to find some shelter whilst we make some sea room so that we have room to manoeuvre should we need to."

"Really Pilot! Are you suggesting that we abandon them to their own devices?"

"It might be their best bet Sir. It's going to get a bit rough out here."

"OK. Hawkins. Send to the junk. Storm force ten expected tonight. Suggest you find shelter amongst the islands if you can. We will move to seaward. See you tomorrow."

"They could use their radio to keep in touch Sir. Leading Tel. Morgan could retune; the nasties won't know."

"Good idea, thank you. Ask Petty Officer Autry to come up to the bridge will you, we'll sort out a frequency for them."

Hawkins spoke down the voicepipe to the wireless office asking that the PO Tel should come up to the bridge to speak to the captain.

*   *   *

"Ship's calling, Bunts."

Petty Officer Barber drew the signalman's attention to the light flashing in Challenger.

"Got 'im, PO"

After a few minutes, he flashed a R for Roger to the ship, put the aldis lamp down and pulled his pencil from his pocket. The signal, when written, was handed to Lieutenant Brothers, leaving the petty officer to wonder what it was about. Serve 'im right for drawing the officer's attention to his not seeing the ship flashing first.

."Find Leading Tel. Morgan, will you, Bunts. Seems they want to establish radio contact so that we can call for help if we need it."

Morgan came up on to the after deck where Lieutenant Brothers and the signalman were standing by the wheel, behind the chicken coop. It had been a considerable advantage to the prize crew that she had been converted from tiller steering to a wheel, presumably when the engines were fitted. Steering such a big vessel with a tiller would have been very hard work though, in heavy weather he suspected, it would be difficult anyway.

Brothers handed him the signal. "What do you think sparks? Can you retune the radio to that frequency?"

"No problem, Sir. Take about five minutes. Bunts can tell them to stand by to receive."

"Challenger this is Prize. How do you hear me? Over."

"This is Challenger. Loud and clear. Wait. Out."

"Prize this is Challenger. Ask Lieutenant Brothers to take the mic please."

Brothers was standing beside the wireless, waiting to hear what the captain had to say.

"Brothers here. Over."

"How are things going? Everything OK?"

"Doctor's diagnosis Sir. As well as can be expected."

"Pilot tells me we are in for a rather nasty night. Storm force ten. Suggest you run for shelter amongst the islands while we get ourselves a little more sea room; too shallow here for comfort. Suggest you keep listening watch on this frequency and transmit only if you need to; with the diesels running you have plenty of power and we won't be too far away. We'll keep you informed of weather prospects. Over."

"Very good Sir. Over."

"This is Challenger. Out."

"Now you see why you were sent with the boarding party Morgan. You might actually make yourself useful."

"I wouldn't want to make a habit of that, Sir. I might get volunteered for too many of these little boating parties. I'm really a big ship sailor. Well, bigger than this, anyway."

*   *   *

Inspector Maple drank his first G&T of the evening. All things considered, it hadn't been too bad a day, Terengganu was really quite a nice posting. Big enough to keep him busy but not big enough to cause any serious problems. The British soldiers had been identified and the army would deal with informing next of kin and all that. There was no indication yet who had killed them or whether the deaths were related at all but time would tell. Sooner or later, all things became known.

They had had a bit of luck with the Chinese girl. She had been identified and her home when searched had provided enough information to show that she was in what passed these days for a relationship with a sergeant who was at the moment in Singapore in hospital. The army would inform him if they wanted him to know. He could see no reason for keeping it from him.

When he came back from the hospital, he would try to find her and, if she wasn't there, he might cause trouble. Better to nip trouble in the bud. Tell the man his paramour was dead; murdered by person or persons unknown. Close the book.

The girl's room had also thrown up the interesting intelligence that she had been married and that her mother in law lived at the south end of town. He had sent a Sergeant and a Constable to see the woman; to explain what had happened. He sipped his drink. Funny. They should have been back by now. Wonder what's keeping them?

The sun was now well down and the temperature falling towards something more acceptable to an Englishman. The humidity was still too high but there was nothing he could do about that. Perhaps, one day, the authorities would install air conditioning but with his luck he would have been retired for years by then.

He wondered again whether, when he retired, he should go home to England. It would be nice but would it be the England that he had left all those years ago? Would he like it? Would he even recognise it?

From what he had heard in letters from relatives, home, England that was, was fast becoming a small version of America with rock and roll bands, youngsters tearing up the seats in cinemas and fighting in the streets. What were they? Teddy boys, Vicky boys? What the hell were they, for God's sake? Perhaps it would be better to stay here, where he understood the system.

Someday, possibly quite soon, Malaya would gain its independence and if he was still in the Force he would be superseded by a local officer. At the moment, almost all the senior officers were English and if Malaya became independent, a Malay government would probably want Malays to be in all the senior positions; that could make things very difficult. At the moment, he knew of no senior Malay officers. All the non-British officers that he knew were Chinese and so were almost all of the sergeants.

Malaysianation was going to be difficult. Unless they were very careful or extraordinarily lucky, there could be a civil war once the British had relinquished control. Perhaps it would be better if he did go home to England after all.

*   *   *

The custom amongst police Inspectors to take a stiff G&T at about this time was not exclusive to Terengganu. In Kota Bahru, Inspector Fredericks had his firmly grasped in his right hand, a matter of inches from his mouth

A Constable knocked on his office door and came in, holding a sheet of paper.

"The Superintendent says to give you this, Sir, it's from military intelligence."

Another knock on the door and Sergeant Lee was there. Fredericks put down the message and glanced up. This was getting like a knocking shop, he told himself when all he wanted was to enjoy his first-of-the-day G&T in peace.

"Evening Lee. You're early."

"Constable Ho just told me what he has found out about the stranger on the wharf, Sir."

"Do you want to tell me or must I ask?"

"The stranger was accommodated at the wharf hotel, charged to Chan Woo's account. Seems he has an account there for visiting captains. But the interesting part is that, later in the day, three more strangers, again Chinese, turned up at Chan Woo's office and were also sent to the hotel at his expense."

"You don't say Lee! Now that makes it interesting." He waved the paper in his hand at Lee. "It seems that, yesterday afternoon, our gallant naval associates arrested a junk smuggling arms and ammunition just down the coast from here. They were careless enough to allow the crew to escape by swimming ashore and legging it into the jungle.

"Now, Lee, what do you think? Could our strangers be the good swimmers referred to in this intelligence?"

"I did say, Sir that the one I saw looked as if his clothes had been wet."

"Actually you described him as dishevelled but you did mention that possibility too, I recall. Right." He put his empty glass down. "I think we had better go and see these strangers. We'd better go mob-handed though, just in case. Sort out a couple or more constables and make sure they're armed."

Lee saluted and went in search of reinforcements. Tonight could be interesting. He would choose some of the more assertive constables, those that were not averse to getting stuck into a fight if necessary. If these strangers turned out to be the smugglers they would probably resist arrest and it would be as well to have the best available help on hand. Lee smiled to himself. To himself he would admit that he quite enjoyed what the English soldiers called a good punch-up; it made him feel young again.

*   *   *

The sky darkened from the south east as the storm approached; the force ten wind driving the sea in front of it, raising the swell to more than twenty feet. Challenger had disappeared, looking for sea room, and to those on the junk the sea looked worse than it had ever done from their ship.

An excellent sea boat, the junk rode the swell without effort but in another hour or so it would be completely dark and Lieutenant Brothers wanted to be tucked up nice and safe behind a nice big island by then.

"Wind her up a bit more Stokes. We'll try a few more knots, see if she will take it in this sea."

Leading Telegraphist Morgan had managed to work out how to switch on the junk's radar and was watching the cursor rotate round the screen, painting the islands ahead.

"The biggest of the islands is about five miles, Sir. Don't know if it's any good to us though. You'll have to look at the chart."

In the tiny cabin, the chart lay on the bunk, held down by four tins of something labelled in Chinese to prevent it rolling itself up.

"No. That won't do. The only bay in which we could try and anchor is on the seaward side. We'll have to try another island."

Morgan couldn't remember the last time he had felt this sick but as the only electrical walla aboard, he was trapped; listening to the radio in case Challenger called and watching the radar hoping to find a nice calm bay in which they could get their heads down until the storm blew itself out or passed on up the coast.

"Now that's interesting," he said to himself. "One of the little islands is moving."

He watched for a few minutes to make doubly sure before reporting it to Lieutenant Brothers.

"I think we have company Sir. Either one of these islands is moving or there's another small vessel trying to do the same as us."

Brothers came down into the cabin to see for himself.

"That one, Sir. I've watched it and it has paused at two of the islands and then moved on. I imagine he is looking for somewhere to shelter too."

"Don't blame him. Keep an eye on him though. Don't want to bump into each other, do we?"

Whilst in the cabin, he took another look at the chart. "Trouble is, we've passed Tioman which would be a good place to hide and I don't really want to back track if I can avoid it. There's three quite large islands and a few small ones in a group just to the south of us. We'll try there. We could be lucky. If that fails, we shall just have to tough it out and continue south towards Singapore."

"The moving island seems to have stopped just to the west of the island behind us. Perhaps he's found shelter there Sir."

"Good luck to him. We'll go on a bit further. He looks very small, doesn't he. "

"Could be just a sampan Sir. Or a small junk."

"Nobody in his right mind would be out here in this weather in a sampan Morgan; any more than we should. The chart suggests that there is a small inlet on the western side of the second island in this group. We'll see what that offers when we get closer. Keep an eye on it, will you. Let me know if it looks promising. Wish we had Challenger's echo sounder."

Morgan watched the cursor painting the islands on the screen; as they grew bigger, a small bay became clearer on the western side, just where the Lieutenant had said it should.

"Three miles to go, Sir. The bay looks big enough but we don't know if its suitable do we?"

"We'll have to revert to old fashioned sailoring Morgan. I wonder if this damned boat has a lead line? Petty Officer Barber," he called through the cabin door. "See if you can improvise a lead line; quick as you can. I imagine the bottom here amongst the islands is suitable for anchoring but we need some idea of the depth of water under our keel."

Some light line was found and a marlinspike tied to the end of it as a sinker. Barber tore his handkerchief into strips and tied them through the line at six-foot intervals. He gave the Lieutenant a wave. "Have to do Sir. Best I can do in the circs."

"Well done PO. It's a bit like the old days, eh? Playing at being real sailors."

"On the whole Sir, I'd rather be on a proper ship and have all the modern kit."

"Have someone in the bows ready to cast that thing over when I tell you, OK?"

They motored slowly towards the entrance of the small bay; more a cleft in the rocks really but it looked as if it might just be big enough for them to creep in and hide from the weather. If so, it would be a perfect place.

"By the mark eight."

The leadsman in the bows called back over his shoulder, hoping that the officer down aft could hear him. If not, those sheltering amidships would pass on his calls.

In amongst the islands the weather was worse; either gusting between them or being suddenly shielded by high-rising almost vertical cliffs. The lightning accompanying the storm flashed almost continuously, illuminating the land that, in its eerie light, seemed at times to be dangerously close.

The first island had been too low to give them any real shelter and the bay shown on the chart was really just an indentation offering no shelter from the wind.

"No good here," Lieutenant Brothers shouted to the Petty Officer standing close beside him. "On we go. Thank God, with the diesels running we can use the radar, eh? I'd hate to try this without it."

On the radar screen, the other vessel was moving again. Morgan had thought it had anchored behind that other island, sheltering from the storm but it was on the move again and it was coming towards them. Why?"

He called up through the skylight to the Lieutenant on the deck above.

"I don't like the look of our friend Sir. I think he's following us."

"Why would anybody do that?"

"Don't know Sir but every time we slow down to take a look-see into a bay, they slow down too. It looks like they're waiting for us to anchor before coming up to us."

"Well, he's out of luck if he's relying on us to lead him into still waters as the Psalm says but you'd better keep an eye on him. Could be a pirate hoping to make a catch, I suppose. To him, we must look like any other junk."

"But how can he see us Sir? Its black as hell out there."

"You think he has radar too, Morgan?"

"If he has he's up to no good, that's for sure."

The full force of the driven sea hit them again as they left what little lee the island had offered. The bow rose to the swell but white water broke over the foc'sle, drenching those on deck.

Almost everybody not actually doing something useful was gathered amidships, holding on to the safety line that stretched from the foremast to the mainmast across the top of the hold. It was not cold, cold by English standards that is, in the ship's waist but it was very wet and uncomfortable. It was, however, the safest place and there they would have to stay until something better offered.

"Damn silly way to make a living, eh bunts?"

Like everyone else, the leading seaman had secured himself by tying a short line round his waist and looping that over the safety line. That way he had two hands free if necessary.

"I think I'll transfer to the army after this, mate."

On the port bow, a darker than dark patch indicated another small island. There seemed to be a lot of these islets, oversized rocks really, too small to provide safe anchorage in their lee.

Lieutenant Brothers having looked at the chart again shouted in the ear of the petty officer. "The next one is bigger, one of the biggest, there looks to be a small cove that might offer shelter."

"I wish we had gone to sea Sir, safer than this with all these small islands. I hope young Morgan is watching out for rocks as well as islands."

"He seems to be interested in another vessel he's got on the radar. Thinks it might be following us but I can't think why it should."

"Perhaps he thinks we know what we're doing, Sir?"

"Could be a pirate of course, we must look like a fat prize which, in this weather, could disappear and nobody would think anything of it."

*   *   *

The Sergeant that had gone to see the dead Chinese girl's mother in law was waiting for his Inspector to return from the lavatory; the first gin always did that to him. The girl's mother in law had told them that her son, who was lying dead on the bed, had come home badly injured and had died in her arms. No, she didn't know anything about the girl's death. Her son had said that he had been attacked by British soldiers; she was going to report it in the morning."

"What do you think Sergeant?"

"He had certainly been stabbed and knocked about a bit; two or three slash wounds and one deep penetration but there's no way I can prove who did it. As her son is the girl's husband, perhaps he was wounded trying to protect her? Personally, I think the old woman was lying but, as both he and the girl are dead, there's nobody left to question, is there Sir?"

"You're probably right Sergeant and, anyway, as you say, there's nobody left to question so, we'll have to close the file on it. All things considered, a nice, neat solution, don't you think?"

"Yes Sir. Very nice, very neat."

"Good. Then I'm off home. Sort out the paperwork will you."

"What about the dead soldiers, Sir?"

"Let the report show that we believe they were murdered by the Chinese man subsequently found dead from his wounds at his mother's house. That should cover it, don't you think?"

The sergeant grinned. His Inspector liked a quiet life and so did he.

"It's raining hard outside Sir, Storm coming I think."

"Then I'll hurry."

*   *   *

When they saw it, illuminated by lightning flashing at just the right moment, the cove looked too small for them to enter but at the minimum revs the junk slid inside.

"By the mark five."

The leadsman in the bows shouted and again threw the weighted line ahead of the ship.

"By the mark four, Sir."

Four fathoms, twenty four feet, plenty for a junk like this but it was obviously shelving rapidly.

"By the mark three."

More a cleft in the rocks, not really a cove, let alone a bay but the almost instant shutting off of the wind and the resulting relative quietness of the water allowed the lieutenant to hear the leadsman's call.

He called down through the skylight to the cabin below. "Tell the stokers to cut the engines."

As the ship drifted slowly further into the sheltering clasp of the cove, the petty officer, now on the tiny foc'sle, let go the anchor. He hoped it would hold. The sudden, almost total silence, here out of the wind allowed normal conversational volume again.

"What do you think, Morgan? Are they still following us?"

"Can't see them now Sir, they're hidden by the side of the cove. At least that means that they can't see us either Sir."

"I think we might turn off all lights and wait and see what happens. PO. Douse all lights, I want a good lookout astern. I want to know immediately if our follower follows us in here."

"Should I arm the lookouts Sir?"

"That shouldn't be necessary PO but have the aldis lamp ready to illuminate the white ensign if necessary. That should be enough to frighten him off if he is a pirate. If he's anyone else, we shall have to deal with that when we know who he is."

Petty Officer Barber left the cabin to organise his lookouts. "Leading Seaman Booker. I want two lookouts stationed on the after deck with binoculars. We're waiting to see if a small vessel that has been following us, follows us in here. If he does, the lieutenant wants you to illuminate the white ensign with the aldis lamp. Do you understand?"

"And what then PO?"

"And then you tell the lieutenant."

"OK PO. I'll organise a watch list."

"And, Booker, if I was you, I'd organise a couple of semi-automatic rifles and a packet or two of shells too but don't say I told you to, OK?"

"Told me to what, PO?"

"That's the spirit. Speaking of which, I think I'll ask Brothers if I can give out a tot all round. I think we've earned it, don't you?"

"Always a good idea PO. Keep the lads happy."

The single cot blanket had been fastened over the missing planks in the cabin's for'ard bulkhead and the lights turned back on. Examination from outside had confirmed that no light showed.

In the cabin, the ship's company, less the two lookouts on deck above them, sat eating corned beef from the tins and drinking their well-earned tot.

"All home comforts, eh PO?"

"Well, at least we're not spewing our rings up now. The wind should have eased by the morning and we can carry on down to Singers."

"PO. Do you think we should advise Challenger of our situation? They could be worried about us."

"Good idea Sir. And about our follower too, if I were you Sir, just in case anything happens. Best if the Senior Officer Present knows the score before the match starts, as you might say."

"He's hardly present but I get your meaning. Morgan. See if you can raise Challenger on the wireless will you." He looked at the chart. "Tell them we're sheltering in the cove on the west side of Mersing Seven and that we appear to have been followed for some time but don't know if our follower is still behind us as we can't see much from where we are."

"Perhaps Challenger's radar can see him Sir. It's a hell of a lot higher up than ours, even if ours wasn't masked by the cliffs."

"Yes, that's an idea. Add a sentence to the effect that any help or advice they can give us would be welcome."

All was quiet on deck; totally dark between the lightning flashes every few seconds and reasonably comfortable for the lookouts. They were wet through but it was hot here out of the wind.

"What do you reckon then, mate?"

"What about? Do I think this other boat will follow us in here? Probably, if he's got any sense, this is the only comfortable berth about, ain't it."

"Suppose so, but what if they start shooting like Hooky said they might?"

"Then we shoots back, you silly bastard. What else?"

"But first we lights up the white ensign so that they know who they are shooting at and exactly where we are? Is that right?"

"That's it mate, that's exactly it."

"Fuck this for a game of soldiers."

"At least we should hear them coming, now its quiet in here."

"It's not quiet out there where they are, stupid. The wind will carry away the sound of their engines."

The sailor lifted the binoculars to his eyes again and waited for the next flash of lightning. Nothing. He lowered the glasses again and relaxed. Perhaps there was nobody out there.

"The sparker could be wrong about us being followed."

"Yes he could but why should he be? It's not as if he's on a bonus, is it?"

"What would he be on a bonus for?"

"For scaring you half to death, that's what."

"Very funny!"

Whilst they were sheltered from the worst of the wind, the rain soaked them through and, lying there on the deck, they were uncomfortable enough to prevent any possibility of going to sleep.

"How long are we on watch for?

"Until the petty officer sends a relief so belt up and enjoy yourself; you're on a free cruise on someone else's yacht, what more do you want?"

In the cabin, sparks was talking to his co-operator in Challenger. "Lieutenant Brothers isn't too bothered about it but I think we've been followed by a small vessel which, to keep us in sight in this weather, must be using radar, so he told me to tell you. Says, can you see anything on your radar as, now that we're hidden in this little bay, ours is shielded and can't see anything.

"Personally, I have a nasty feeling about it. I mean, why would anyone want to follow us and, how many small boats have radar?"

"OK. I'll make sure the Old Man knows you're worried. Challenger out."

*   *   *

"What d'you think Harry?"

"I don't know Sir but Petty Officer Primrose tells me that he can't see anything moving amongst the islands."

The captain pushed the bell for his steward. "Ask the navigating officer to step in, will you Masters. You can tell him its urgent."

He indicated a chair to the first lieutenant. "I think we had better assume that something is up, even if we don't know what it is."

"You wanted me, Sir?"

"Ah, Pilot. We seem to have a problem. Our junk thinks they have been followed by a small vessel which, to do so, must be fitted with radar. Any ideas?"

"There can't be two junks out there with radar, surely Sir."

"Then what are we left with? I suppose it could be a pirate. Do they have radar, do you know? You'd better have a look at the chart and see if we can get in amongst the islands in the dark and in this weather. Doesn't appeal but we'd better look into it just in case. If, as they say, their radar can't see the follower, than I imagine their follower cant see them, so they are safe enough for the moment. I think I'd like to be up with them by first light.

"Sort something out will you between you. Let me know what I'm to do and when."

TWENTY

Morning finally came in the tiny cleft in which they were anchored. There had been no sign of the follower during the night; a fact for which the succession of lookouts had been duly grateful.

The watchers could smell the breakfast bacon frying and hear the rest of the hands moving about either on deck or in the cabin below them.

Dawn had not been visible from inside the cove in which they sheltered but the sky above them was light now and the heavy grey clouds had passed.

"Looks like we may have survived the tempest, eh?"

"Yes mate but we still have to get to Singers before I'll be happy."

Lieutenant Brothers climbed the steps from the welldeck. "No sign of them, then?"

"No Sir."

"Right. We'll be off as soon as we've fed. No hurry really and the sea outside will still be quite rough."

As all their meals had been since boarding, breakfast was a sandwich, bacon this time; they would all be happy to get ashore and get a proper meal inside them. At least bacon made a change from the corned beef that had been their staple diet for the last few days.

With their attention focused on the chef, the source of the aroma so delighting their nostrils, the lookouts didn't see the large police launch stand in to the entrance of the cove. The first they knew of it was the sound of a heavy machine gun spraying bullets across the after deck on which they were standing. Able Seaman Andrews fell, clutching at Signalman Sallis and bringing him down too, thus saving his life.

There was no need to warn the others. They had heard the shooting and felt the impact of the heavy, probably twenty millimetre, bullets hitting the ship.

"Grab that gun and give me a hand," Sallis shouted to the nearest man. He threw off the still body of Bob Andrews and took aim over the stern of the ship, letting rip with a long burst which seemed to dampen the enemy's enthusiasm for a moment. The silence seemed to go on for ever before a voice was heard from the Bullhorn on the police launch.

"This is the police, put up your arms, you are under arrest."

Lieutenant Brothers, whilst thinking it a little odd that the police launch would shout in English to what must appear to be a Chinese junk, shouted back, "We are the Royal Navy. Cease fire."

The launch responded by firing another long burst killing many of the chickens in the chicken coop in front of which the lookouts lay flat on the deck.

All but the two armed lookouts, who were unable to move without being seen, had taken shelter for'ard of the cabin and were protected by it but they were not idle.

"PO. Can you see the launch from your side? I can't see it from here!"

"Yes Sir but he's got us outgunned. That there sounds like a twenty millimetre and with that he can stand off and hit anything that moves."

"That's an idea PO. We could invite him to waste quite a bit of ammunition if we let the chickens fly, he's not killed all of them. With luck he'll shoot at anything that moves before realising that he's just wasting ammunition."

The Petty Officer crawled up the steps keeping his head well down and slithered along the deck. Four or five birds had survived the initial onslaught and he lifted what was left of the coop off the deck, shooing them out on to the deck from which they immediately tried to flap away from the supposed danger, the PO.

The movement was seen and another burst of machinegun fire sprayed the deck. The whine of bullets ricocheting from the radar scanner inside the coop added a little realism to an otherwise totally ridiculous situation. "Fuck this for a game of soldiers!"

Leading Seaman Booker grabbed two of the others and told them to help him unlash the cover of the hold.

"What we going to do then Hooky? Hide 'til they get tired and go home?"

"No you prat, we're going to see what the Chinese Government has provided in the way of armaments. Now, get yourself down there and start moving that timber out of our way."

Lieutenant Brothers saw the men start to uncover the hold.

"What are you up to Booker?"

"Seeing if there's anything down there to shoot back with, Sir. Our Lanchesters are all very well for quelling a riot, lots of noise and not much impact, but they're no bloody use against that twenty millimetre I can hear back there."

"Good idea, shake it about a bit down there, we may need whatever you find quite quickly if they decide to come alongside."

On the after deck the two lookouts let fly with another fusillade, knowing that it was pure bravado; not the slightest chance of doing any serious harm to their adversary.

*   *   *

"Bridge, Plot. I think I saw the junk's follower just now but she's gone behind the island. They should be able to see the junk from where they are."

"Bridge, wireless office. Junk reports under attack by police launch. Says they have identified themselves to the launch but are under fire from what sounds like a twenty millimetre heavy machine gun."

Yeoman Houser repeated the message to the officer of the watch.

"Captain Sir. Junk reports it's under attack by a police launch. Says they have identified themselves to the police but are still under attack."

"I'll be right up."

The first lieutenant closed the lid of the voicepipe to the captain's cabin.

"Morning Number One. Trouble, then."

"It would seem so Sir. Why would a police launch attack them, do you think? After they have told them who they are."

231

The captain returned the first lieutenant's salute.

"Perhaps the police didn't believe them Harry. The Royal Navy do not habitually sail round the South China Sea in junks. What's the course for their hiding place?"

"We're on our way, Sir. Should be able to see it in ten minutes I should think."

The captain leant over the voicepipe to the wheelhouse. "Wheelhouse. Revs for thirty knots."

On the bridge they could hear the revs being wound on to the rev counter that communicated with the engineroom. The bell clanged, indicating that the engineroom had acknowledged and repeated back the instruction.

"Three hundred and ten revs repeated, Sir."

"Thank you. Now, Harry, let's see what sort of a fist we make of emulating the famous seventh cavalry."

"This doesn't sound like an American cowboy film to me Sir. Action Stations?"

"Yes please. Just in case, eh?"

The first lieutenant hit the red knob of the klaxon, immediately in front of him. The sound reverberated throughout the ship, interrupting the breakfasts in most of the messes.

"Bloody typical, ain't it! I thought this was supposed to be a nice peaceful cruise down to Singers and then home for me. I think the bastards are trying to kill me so that I can't go."

Bob Arthur's bleat was received with good humour by his messmates, everybody knew that he was on his way home once they got to Singapore. He had done his two and a half years and his relief should be in HMS Terror waiting to join.

"Shift your arse Bob, the captain's depending on you to defend his ship. Wonder what this is all about, eh?"

At 310 revs, the whole ship vibrated, everything not tightly tied down rattled and, on the chart table under the forebridge canopy, the parallel rules rolled over the chart and into the trough provided for them as the ship healed to the turn.

Throughout the ship, gun's crews tested all circuits, raised and lowered the barrels and checked the traverse of their weapons. Additional lookouts closed up on the bridge and the first lieutenant nodded to the captain and went below to his action station in the damage control centre.

Looking aft, the captain could see the foaming white wake building up as the ship's speed increase until, after only a few minutes, the wake formed a wall of white water immediately astern of the ship and higher than the quarterdeck that it followed.

It was back. That feeling of excitement that always followed the sounding of the action stations klaxon. His heart was pumping again, he could feel the adrenalin coursing through his veins as the needle on the speed indicator wound round further with each extra knot achieved. It wouldn't be long now; five minutes? Perhaps less. It depended upon what the aggressor was doing.

He had no way of knowing which way round the island would be best but, in any event, the so-called police launch was unable to see their approach and their sudden arrival on the field of battle would instantly reverse any advantage they had held until that moment.

*　　*　　*

233

"Well? What have you found down there? And, have we any ammunition for it?"

Leading Seaman Booker's search party below passed a long box up through the gap in the hold cover. "Hang about Hooky, I've seen the ammo for that here somewhere."

"Christ! A bleeding Bazooka! Now that's what I call useful." He leant over the hold again. "Chop chop down there."

He turned to the lieutenant. "Won't take long now, Sir. What if we was to stop returning their fire? Do you think they might risk coming alongside for a looksee? If we can hit him with this beauty, we could do some serious damage. Might even up the odds a bit, Sir."

Brothers looked at Petty Officer Barber, raising one eyebrow in question. "What do you think PO? Worth a try? Of course, if they get alongside and there's more of them than there is of us, we could be in a certain amount of trouble."

"Worth a try Sir. We don't have to let them come right alongside, just close enough for that bloody rocket thingy to cause mayhem. What's the range of one of them things Hooky?"

"No idea PO, they're for taking out tanks and things. Don't have a lot of call for them at sea."

The lookouts called down from above them that the launch was moving away, leaving.

"Thank you. Keep me informed."

"What do you think PO?"

"Just going for his breakfast Sir. He'll be back."

"What makes you so sure?"

"Well, Sir. If they was real police, they would have argued the toss with us about us being Royal Navy. We have the white ensign on the staff where they can see it. No. I reckon they're the enemy trying to get their guns back."

"Well PO, as they are shooting at us, they are the enemy as far as I'm concerned, whoever they are really. They've killed one of my men and I want my revenge. How about we up anchor and try to reverse out of here? If we can put some sea room between us we may be able to out run them."

"Worth a try, Sir. We're a sitting duck in here. Also, if they are the enemy wanting their guns back, they won't want to sink us out there, will they? Only while if we're somewhere where they can be sure of getting to the wreck, eh?"

"Right. Get that anchor up as soon as I've got the engines working. Stokes! Get the engines working, I want us out of here before that maniac comes back."

The two stokers dived down below.

*   *   *

"How long, Pilot?"

Challenger was moving through the still quite rough sea at more than thirty knots, far faster than she should have been but taking it very well. The sea was behind her, helping her along and the swell was much less than it had been the night before.

"Few minutes, Sir. Nothing on radar but of course there wouldn't be if they're both behind the island."

"Guns?"

"All closed up Sir. Will you want the four point fives, do you think?"

"Probably Guns. The Bofors should be enough to despatch a police launch but you never know in this world, we'll keep them closed up."

"Yeoman. Get the wireless office to tell the junk that we're on our way. Should be with them any minute now."

The captain was enjoying himself. Action, action in which there was very little real risk of damage to his ship, would do the ship's company no harm. Teach them that there was no such thing as peace for a warship.

*   *   *

The throb of the junk's diesels echoed back from the walls of the cove as she reversed at full revs out towards the sea. It was unlikely that the junk had ever moved quite that quickly backwards but she was well built and took it well.

Lying prone on the tiny foc'sle, Petty Officer Barber waited. A few boxes of rifles had been lifted out of the hold too and used to build a low, protecting wall behind which he lay.

"Any minute now PO." Lieutenant Brothers was standing beside the wheel, a prime target if the launch got their shots in first. "When we get to the entrance, I'm going to swing her round and get the head pointing towards Singapore. It'll take a moment for the engines to move into full ahead and that should give you a moment of almost stillness in which to aim and fire that thing."

The petty officer looked over his shoulder to where the lieutenant was standing. "Aye aye, Sir, as they used to say in the old navy. Christ, this is more like C.S. Forrester than Douglas Reeman, ain't it."

A smile spread over the lieutenant's face. "It's largely his fault I'm in the navy, PO. He was one of my teenage heroes; well Hornblower was; never thought I'd find myself in this sort of situation in the nineteen fifties!"

He wound the wheel hard over as they broke out of the cove, the stern slewed round to bring the bow facing the direction in which the launch had disappeared.

The bazooka kicked like a mule as the rocket left it, aimed at the launch which was, at that moment, turning to intercept. The launch's wheelhouse disintegrated. "Christ, this thing's good, ain't it!"

A second rocket was fed into the mouth of the tube and Leading Seaman Booker tapped the PO on the shoulder to confirm that his weapon was reloaded.

The machinegun on the launch stuttered and wood chips flew off the boxes behind which Barber and Booker were lying, making them keep their heads down.

The second rocket missed and was roundly cursed by both seamen. "Quick, Hooky, reload."

On the wheel, the steersman was blind. "Chop chop up there. I can't see where I'm steering from down where I'm lying PO."

The tap on his shoulder let Petty Officer Barber raise his head again and take quick aim at the launch, which was lying broadside on to them now. The hit on the wheelhouse must have destroyed the steering but they were still shooting at the junk.

"Good shot mate! Fucking good shot."

The whole front end of the launch opened up like a flower, parts of it flying high into the air and landing near the approaching junk.

"Wasn't me, for Christ's sake. I haven't fired."

Challenger slewed round the end of the island behind the launch and a second four point five inch shell hit what was left of it. Her wake, standing up behind her at speed, fell away as Challenger slowed, her tall, sharp bow pushing to one side the few planks of wood still afloat.

Barber leapt to his feet and waved at the ship.

"Watch you don't shoot anybody with that thing PO, you'd have a hard time explaining that away. Could cost you your rate."

"Yeah, reckon it could eh. What a sight though eh?"

"Junk ahoy." The loud hailer on the side of Challenger's bridge broke into life. "Good morning. Heard you were having a little trouble with the local gendarmerie. Trust all is now in order?"

Lieutenant Brothers stood up and waved his hat. "Good morning Sir. Didn't expect you quite this early but you're very welcome none the less."

"You'd better bring that thing alongside. You look like you could all do with a nice cup of tea."

*   *   *

Wireless communication with C in C in Singapore elicited the information that a police launch had been stolen in Kuantan two days ago and, according to the CinC, the police were not going to be at all happy about Challenger sinking their boat.

However, it was good to know that the junk and its cargo were safe.

*   *   *

Once more in convoy, as it were, the two ships had cruised at reduced speed towards Singapore and the naval base. The dead able seaman had been washed and laid out on the bunk in the junk's after cabin, ready to be passed over to Challenger for refrigerated storage and, eventually, ashore for a full military funeral.

"Bloody hard luck that, weren't it!"

Telegraphist Morgan, being of little use on deck, had been detailed to clean up the dead man and wrap him in the only thing available, the blanket that had previously been used as a temporary for'ard bulkhead for the cabin.

He nodded, silently. The two stokers were in the cabin with him, listening to the diesels' steady throb. "When do you reckon they'll transfer him back to the ship?"

"The signal said to have him ready before sunset. Then they can dip the ensign when he comes over the side."

"Reckon we'll get an extra tot when we take him back onboard? "

Sparks smiled, nodding at the body on the bunk. "Well, if we do, I want his! It's the least he can do for me after all I've done for him."

On deck, Petty Officer Barber watched the sunset. Able Seaman Andrews' body had been passed across to Challenger covered by a pristine white ensign and the ensign at

Challenger's stern had been dipped in respect. "You can always tell when you're near Singapore," he told the ordinary seaman standing beside him. "There's an electrical storm over Singapore Island every night, regular as clockwork. Not like the one we saw last night but quite impressive. You've never been to Singapore, have you? Joined us in Hong Kong didn't you? Well, we'll be in by tomorrow afternoon thank God, I could do with a run ashore and a pint!"

"Me too."

EPILOGUE

Darling Sweetheart,

We finally managed to capture the junk we had been sent to find and arrest and set course for Singapore, thinking that it was all over bar the shouting.

However, this morning, we had to sink an armed police launch that had been stolen by communist terrorists and with which they were trying to recapture the junk; we had been separated in some rather bad weather.

The prize crew we had put aboard the junk made a stout defence, although initially outgunned by the launch's twenty millimetre heavy machine gun but they had the good sense to break into the cargo of arms that the junk was carrying for the terrorists and found, would you believe(?) a bazooka, hand-held, anti-tank rocket-launcher!

To be honest, I don't know for sure whether it was their rocket or our 4.5 inch shells that did for the launch but anyway, it all came right in the end thank God. We did lose one man killed by the enemy's fire and I shall have to write to his wife and explain how I came to lose her husband; not a job I relish at all, never have: though I've had to do it several times in the past. I thought that was all over in '45 but there you are.

Tomorrow, we shall be in Singapore and I shall post this letter. I will write to you again in the next few days, after I have spoken to the admiral and his minions to confirm that it would be possible for you to join me out here. My first

Lieutenant, Harry Enders whom you have not met, is arranging for his fiancé to join him here so that they may be married. He suggests that, if we can arrange it, you two girls could perhaps come out together, keeping each other company during the long voyage.

You have no idea how much I miss you and want you here with me, even if later they send me back to Korea. Our refit will take at least three to four months; they seem to want to install all sorts of new anti-aircraft radar and things as they think this will be different kind of war from the last one that was largely anti-submarine; the old lady just won't look the same but I suppose that's progress.

If I know the navy, they'll probably spend a lot of money on her, finish the refit late and then decide to scrap the old girl as surplus to requirements or unsuitable for future warfare or something like that. I do hope not, she is a good ship for all her faults and we have a good ship's company. I would like to think that we can stay together for a while longer.

If my plan works out with the admiral, I'll send you Harry Enders' fiancé's telephone number and you can get together and arrange things at your end. You have no idea just how much I miss you; letters just aren't the same, although I read yours two or three times each.

Take care of yourself and stay happy,
All my love,

David